Zoe gazed down at the dog. "She's beautiful."

"And intelligent and trained to be lethal, if necessary," Linc cautioned.

"I don't doubt that for a second." Meeting Star's upturned face with a tender look of her own, Zoe dangled the tips of her fingers over the edge of the box. The dog noticed but didn't seem upset, so she took a chance and wiggled them.

Star had apparently realized she wasn't a danger because she sniffed Zoe's fingers, then gave them a quick lick.

"Are you trying to recruit her to the dark side?"

"Not at all. Actually, I'm very impressed with Star. She's a lot smarter than you security forces people are. She's already decided I'm one of the good guys around here."

"Then it's a good thing she's not the one in charge."

* * *

MILITARY K-9 UNIT:
These soldiers track down a serial killer
with the help of their brave canine partners

Valerie Hansen was thirty when she awoke to the presence of the Lord in her life and turned to Jesus. She now lives in a renovated farmhouse in the breathtakingly beautiful Ozark Mountains of Arkansas and is privileged to share her personal faith by telling the stories of her heart for Love Inspired. Life doesn't get much better than that!

Books by Valerie Hansen

Love Inspired Suspense

Military K-9 Unit

Bound by Duty

Classified K-9 Unit

Special Agent

Rookie K-9 Unit

Search and Rescue
Rookie K-9 Unit Christmas
"Surviving Christmas"

The Defenders

Nightwatch
Threat of Darkness
Standing Guard
A Trace of Memory
Small Town Justice
Dangerous Legacy

Visit the Author Profile page at Harlequin.com for more titles.

BOUND BY DUTY

VALERIE HANSEN

HARLEQUIN® LOVE INSPIRED® SUSPENSE

Special thanks and acknowledgment are given to Valerie Hansen
for her contribution to the Military K-9 Unit miniseries.

Recycling programs
for this product may
not exist in your area.

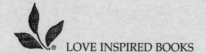

LOVE INSPIRED BOOKS

ISBN-13: 978-1-335-49034-6

Bound by Duty

Copyright © 2018 by Harlequin Books S.A.

www.Harlequin.com

Printed in U.S.A.

God is our refuge and strength, a very present help in trouble. Therefore we will not fear.

–Psalms 46:1-2

Special thanks to former air force sergeant Nancy N. for her advice and to our pastor, John, who also served, as did his son.

Terri Reed, Dana Mentink, Maggie K. Black, Lenora Worth, Lynette Eason, Laura Scott, Shirlee McCoy and I all did our best to support each other's efforts and learn proper air force protocol for this series. It was difficult, but we gave it our all.

God bless the men and women of our current military who daily give far more and those who have sacrificed in the past to keep us free. We are grateful beyond words.

ONE

She was being watched. Constantly. Every fiber of her being knew it. Lately, she felt as though she was the defenseless prey and packs of predators were circling her and her helpless little boy, which was why she'd left Freddy at home with a sitter. Were things as bad as they seemed? It was more than possible, and Staff Sergeant Zoe Sullivan shivered despite the warm spring day.

Scanning the busy parking lot as she left the Canyon Air Force Base Exchange with her purchases, Zoe quickly spotted one of the Security Forces investigators. Her pulse jumped, and hostility took over her usually amiable spirit. The K-9 cop in a blue beret and camo ABU—Airman Battle Uniform—was obviously waiting for her. She bit her lip. Nobody cared how innocent she was. Being the half sister of Boyd Sullivan, the escaped Red Rose Killer, automatically made her a person of interest.

Zoe clenched her teeth. There was no way she could prove herself, so why bother trying? She squared her slim shoulders under her blue off-duty T-shirt and stepped out, heading straight for the Security Forces man and his imposing K-9, a black-and-rust-colored rottweiler.

Clearly, he saw her coming because he tensed, feet

apart, body braced. In Zoe's case, five and a half feet was the height she could muster. The dark-haired tech sergeant she was approaching looked to be quite a bit taller.

He gave a slight nod as she drew near and greeted her formally. "Sergeant Sullivan."

Linc Colson's firm jaw, broad shoulders and strength of presence were familiar. They had met during a questioning session conducted by Captain Justin Blackwood and Master Sergeant Westley James shortly after her half brother had escaped from prison.

Zoe stopped and gave the cop an overt once-over. "Can I help you with something, Sergeant Colson?"

"No, ma'am."

A cynical smile teased at one corner of her mouth. "Oh? Then why is it you're always following me? Don't you ever get a day off?"

"Just doing my job, Sergeant."

She knew he was right, but it galled her to be the object of futile efforts when base Security Forces could have been using their manpower to figure out who at Canyon Air Force Base was *really* cooperating with Boyd. How long were they going to continue disrupting her life and work? A wryly humorous thought intruded, and she chuckled.

Colson stared. The muscular K-9 at his side tensed. "What's so funny?"

Zoe waved her hands in dismissal as best she could with the canvas grocery tote handles looped over her forearms. "Relax, Sergeant. I wasn't laughing at you. I was just picturing you guys trying to track me when I'm giving flying lessons. How are you at piloting a T-38 in close formation?"

She was relieved to note he was having difficulty containing his own smile. His mouth stayed put, but there was no denying a spark in his green eyes.

"I'd wait for you on the ground," he said. "Or outside the simulator."

Sobering, Zoe shook her head slowly, her light brown ponytail swinging. "I don't suppose it would do me any good to take an oath that I haven't seen Boyd since the last time I visited him in prison."

"That's not for me to say."

"No, I don't suppose it is." An eyebrow arched above her hazel eyes. "What if it were? Would you be willing to at least give me the benefit of the doubt instead of condemning me outright?"

To her surprise and disappointment, he said, "No."

"So much for the famous air force camaraderie," Zoe muttered. Louder, she said, "Fine," shouldered past him and started up the sidewalk toward Base Boulevard.

He turned slightly as she passed. "Those bags look heavy. Why didn't you call a cab after you bought so much?"

"It's a beautiful spring day in the heart of Texas," she snapped back. "Walking is a pleasure."

"If you say so."

Righteous indignation surged, and she picked up her pace. She couldn't stop the base cops from shadowing her, but she didn't have to make it easy. If her conscience hadn't kept kicking up, she would have enjoyed her impromptu plan to ditch this one even more.

Instead of looking back to see how far ahead she was getting, she checked the reflections in the rear window of a bus that was unloading green recruits, probably for a tour of the impressive shopping facilities at the Base Exchange.

It looked as if Sergeant Colson was trailing her by at least a hundred yards. *Good.* Her smile returned. She shouldered her way through the milling group of men and women gathered on the sidewalk, then ducked in front of the idling bus, keeping it between her and the K-9 cop for as long as she could before darting around the far end of the stores in the Exchange and breaking into a run.

The moment she saw the warehouse complex behind the stores she knew exactly what to do next. She slipped between two of them and paused to catch her breath. Yes, the K-9 could and would track her. But in the meantime, she intended to enjoy thwarting his handler for a few minutes. Let Colson wonder where she was and what she was up to. Base personnel had already painted her as a clever criminal, a person to be avoided and mistrusted. A contrary side to her nature insisted on payback.

She ducked around a second corner, tried a side door to one of the warehouse buildings, found it unlocked and bolted through, lowering her sacks of groceries to the floor as she pressed her back to the inside of the steel door.

Breathless, Zoe stared into the darkness of the vast windowless storage area and waited for her night vision to improve.

This is wrong, her conscience insisted.

Was she finished playing games? *Not quite.* Leaving behind her purchases, she flipped the lock on the door to secure it and began to edge past pallets of boxes stacked in rows, looking for a different exit.

The sudden whirring of a motor stopped her in her tracks. Somebody was raising the overhead bay doors at the far end. Light crept below the broad edge of the moving panels. Then they stopped, leaving a gap of about three feet between the floor and the base of the door.

Zoe didn't move. Hardly breathed. Had Sergeant Colson located her already? Wow, he was good at tracking. Or, at least, his dog was. She was preparing to step forward and reveal herself—until she realized she wasn't seeing a K-9.

Instead, a man in camo and combat boots and a woman wearing a skirt and high heels ducked beneath the hanging door. All Zoe could see clearly was their feet and lower legs, but it was obvious she'd given Colson too much credit. He hadn't found her. This was probably nothing more than a lovers' tryst.

Voices reached her but were too muted to understand. She was about to back away and give the couple privacy when she saw a muzzle flash and heard the reverberation of a gunshot.

Instinct made her duck and cover her ears. Self-preservation kept her down while every hair at the nape of her neck prickled and her body trembled, willing her to run yet keeping her feet leaden. She could barely breathe.

The female figure was crumpling to the floor. Zoe could see blood spreading across the back of a reddish-haired woman's light-colored blouse. The shooter bent over her, his gun at the ready, a black ski mask hiding his features.

Help! She had to get help. Trembling, Zoe pulled her cell phone from the pocket of her PT shorts. Its lit screen and beeps of dialing were her undoing. As the victim lay still, bleeding and perhaps dying, the assailant straightened, wheeled to face the noise and started to move toward Zoe.

He was coming for her. She was next!

Linc Colson was concentrating, his jaw clenched, every nerve taut, as he followed K-9 Star. The rottweiler was as good as they came, and he trusted her tracking skills implicitly. That was why when she began to bark and paw at a closed warehouse door, he drew his sidearm and immediately tried the handle. Locked. And far too sturdily made to kick open.

He'd reached for the mic clipped to his shoulder, intending to report the evasive actions of his assigned suspect when a C-130 passing overhead forced a delay. He could hardly hear Star's barking over the roar of those engines, let alone hope to be able to transmit clearly. He just hoped Sergeant Sullivan hadn't run off to meet her murderous brother.

Linc jiggled the door handle again to no avail. He had just let it go when the heavy door swung open and a body slammed into his chest. *Zoe Sullivan!* Pushing her away, he commanded Star to sit and stay while one hand hovered over his holster and he faced his quarry.

Gasping, she raised both hands, palms out. "Don't shoot. It's me."

"I can see that." He had to shout at her to make himself heard over the fading roar of the cargo plane.

When she reached out to him, he took additional evasive action. "Stay where you are."

"No! You don't understand."

Her voice was shrill. Different than before. She

sounded frightened. Well, too bad. "If you didn't want to get in more trouble, you shouldn't have tried to ditch me." He peered past her. "Where's Boyd?"

"How should I know?"

Judging by the way she kept shaking her head, waving her hands and gaping at him, she'd scared herself more than she'd worried him. Good. It served her right.

"I'm sorry. I promise I won't do it again, but…"

"You sure won't." He signaled his dog to stand guard. "No more special courtesy for you, Sergeant Sullivan. From now on, I'm your shadow. You got that?"

"Fine. Then follow me."

She turned and ducked back through the open door so quickly only Star kept up. Linc shouted, "Stop!" But the flight instructor kept right on going, stumbling when Star got in front of her to try to block her progress.

Linc grabbed a fistful of the back of Zoe's shirt and yanked her back outside. "Oh, no, you don't!"

She struggled against his hold. "Let me go. She may not be dead yet!"

"*Who* may not be dead? What kind of games are you playing now?"

"No games. I saw a woman get shot." Staggering to keep her balance, she pointed with her whole arm. "Right in there. The shot echoed. You must have heard it, too."

"Not over the engines of a C-130." Linc drew his gun and took a defensive stance. "If you're lying…"

"I'm not. I saw the shooting with my own eyes. When I tried to phone for help, the killer spotted me. I had to run for my life." Her lips trembled. "And, no, it wasn't Boyd. At least not this time."

Either the flight instructor was telling the truth or she

deserved an Oscar for acting, Linc decided. Not only was she shaking all over, his own nerves had begun firing wildly. The back of his neck tingled and he sensed danger the way he had in combat when trying to outwit a hidden enemy.

Pushing her aside with his free arm, he aimed blindly into the dark warehouse. "How could you see a thing in there?"

"The—the loading door at the other end was partly open when it all happened. The guy must have closed it after he shot her."

Linc reached for his radio, reported the possible crime and was assured of backup, then instructed Zoe. "You stay out here. I'm going in to see if I can find the lights."

"No way. Suppose the shooter gets behind you."

"Star would alert me."

"I still think I should go along. I can help."

"The dog can do it better," Linc insisted.

"I give up. I'm scared, okay? My little boy needs me, and you know I'm unarmed. The shooter knows I saw him. I don't want to wait out here by myself."

He could hear her rapid breathing, feel her fear. "That's the first totally honest thing I've heard you say," Linc replied. "All right. But stay close behind me in case I have to fire."

"Gladly."

Stepping inside, Linc placed each boot as silently as possible. He moved ahead in a half crouch in order to present a smaller target. Star preceded him. Zoe followed.

A swishing, fluttering noise from above startled all three of them. Zoe let out a tiny gasp but didn't scream, impressing him, despite his lingering anger at her foolish tricks. Star paused for a moment, then looked forward again. "A bird in the rafters," Linc whispered.

Although his human companion didn't react, he continued to feel her presence, as if his actual shadow had substance. He'd have waited for backup if Sullivan hadn't mentioned a victim. Given that complication, he needed to reach the scene and assess any injuries. Quickly.

Pausing, Linc waved his palm in front of Star's nose, then held it up to stop Zoe, too. "Stay here. The panel for the lights is right ahead. When I turn them on, I don't want you to be out in the open."

"Will your dog panic and bite me if you leave?" Zoe whispered.

Under other circumstances Link would have chuckled. "Not unless I tell her to, so don't run away again."

Sergeant Sullivan's muttered reply faded to nothing as Linc moved forward. His sight had adjusted to the darkness enough to tell where he was but not enough to spot hidden attackers.

He reached for the panel and flipped the switches. Banks of overhead fluorescent lights flickered, then steadied, illuminating the entire warehouse.

Linc's first act was to ensure that there was no imminent threat. His gaze swept the building contents, then came to rest on Zoe. Star was seated at her feet, panting and totally unconcerned, meaning she sensed no danger lurking nearby.

In contrast, the flight instructor was standing there with her hazel eyes wide and her mouth hanging open, looking as though she was about to keel over.

Linc followed her line of sight to the base of the roll-up door. The concrete was spotless.

No dust.

No blood stain.

And no body.

TWO

Zoe took a shaky breath. "That's impossible!" She wanted to explain what had happened but couldn't. She had seen the shooting with her own eyes. Had watched the victim fall and bleed. So where had the injured woman gone?

Her companion reached for his mic. "Colson here. False alarm at the warehouse."

Watching his expression removed all doubt that he blamed her for the false alarm. Only it wasn't her fault. It hadn't been. She knew what she'd seen, how she'd felt when the assailant had turned and come toward her. Imagination or hallucination or whatever a person wanted to call it was not enough to scare her that much.

The K-9 handler raised a dark eyebrow. "Well?"

"Oh, no. You're not going to blame me for this, Colson. I don't know what really happened, but I am not making anything up. I heard a shot. I saw a victim fall and watched a red stain blossom on her back. There is no way this floor can be this clean and dry after that. Not this fast. There has to be a logical explanation."

"I'm waiting for it," he said.

Zoe took a deep breath and exhaled noisily. Slowly shaking her head, she glanced down at the imposing patrol K-9. "I'd rather try to explain it to your dog. She looks more likely to believe me."

"Don't let her temporary relaxation fool you. One word or signal from me and Star will be a formidable adversary."

"I know. It's just that sometimes I tend to relate to animals better than I do humans. And see her cute tan eyebrows? She's not scowling at me the way you are."

"Maybe that's because you didn't lie to her."

"I didn't lie to you either." Zoe knew there was pathos in her tone, but she didn't try to hide or excuse it. "There has to be a clue here. A drop of blood or something. Please. Bring in somebody who can test the area for it. At least give me the benefit of the doubt."

"So you can waste our time and resources?"

Her voice became strident. "*Me?* You're the ones who are wasting time by focusing on *my* life when you should be trying to track down my stupid half brother before he does something else too horrible for words. I haven't seen him since before he escaped, and I only went because I felt sorry for him. I don't want to see him on the outside of prison walls. I have my little boy to protect. Do you think I want Boyd anywhere near Freddy?"

"Why not? You sure visited him plenty."

"That's different. Boyd's all the family I have left since Dad died. I suppose I should have stayed away, but I kept hoping he was worth redeeming."

"By you?" She heard him huff.

"No. By God and Jesus," Zoe said, and this time there was new gentleness in her speech.

"Some people aren't worth it," Colson countered drily.

"I disagree. *Everybody* should have the chance to reform, no matter what they've done." Her heart clenched. Too bad it was too late to help Freddy's daddy.

That all-encompassing statement apparently convinced the cop to turn away and once again use his radio. "Give me Captain Blackwood," he said. After a short pause he followed with, "Linc Colson here, sir. I'm at warehouse W-16 behind the BX. Sullivan insists she saw a crime committed and is requesting a tech team. Do you want me to stay here until you give me further orders or shall I relinquish the scene?"

Zoe couldn't hear the reply because the sergeant was wearing an earpiece, but judging by his grim look, he wasn't happy with the captain's decision. She waited expectantly for him to end the call and explain.

"They're coming," he grumbled. "You win. This time."

"I'm not trying to win anything," she insisted. "I just don't want a criminal to get away with murder."

"Right."

Zoe could have brought up the sacrifice of personal happiness she'd made when she'd turned in her former husband, John, for possible espionage, a transgression, which may have been responsible for his untimely death, but since those records were sealed, she figured it would be best to keep that part of her past to herself. Her rotten brother was plenty for now. Between relatives she couldn't help knowing and choosing the wrong man to marry, her record of discernment was pitiful.

She decided to try changing the subject. "So, Linc is what the *L* on your name tag stands for? Is that short for Lincoln?"

"Not anymore. It's just Linc now."

"Why?"

"Because I got tired of being called Abe. Nicknames are bad enough in the air force. They were lots worse when I was a kid."

She had to smile at him. "Gotcha. Boyd liked to call me Baby Sister, and the kids in the neighborhood and at school picked it up. Thankfully, it didn't follow me into the air force, even if my brother did."

"You got off easy when he washed out." He gestured to some cardboard cartons piled near the open bay doors. "We might as well sit down."

"Your *dog* is tired, right?"

One corner of his mouth twitched for a moment as if a smile was trying to get out before he regained control and answered, "Right. My *partner* is."

"Sorry." Zoe led the way to the stack and tested it to make sure the carton was strong enough to support her before sitting. "I had forgotten you guys considered your K-9s partners."

Linc took a seat with Star between them. "We're classified as teammates. She's an MWD, Military Working Dog, and I'm her handler."

Zoe gazed down. "She's beautiful."

"And intelligent and trained to be lethal if necessary," Linc cautioned.

"I don't doubt that for a second." Meeting Star's upturned face with a tender look of her own, Zoe dangled the tips of her fingers over the edge of the box. The dog noticed but didn't seem upset, so she took a chance and wiggled them.

Star had apparently realized she wasn't a danger, because she sniffed Zoe's fingers, then gave them a quick lick.

Zoe giggled. Linc did not. "It's a good thing for you that Star has been socialized more than some of our other dogs or she'd never put up with that. What are you trying to do, recruit her over to the dark side?"

That opinion deserved a hearty laugh. "Not at all. Actually, I'm very impressed with Star. She's a lot smarter than you Security Forces people are. She's already decided I'm one of the good guys around here."

"Then it's a good thing she's not the one in charge."

Linc was not pleased by Zoe's conclusion, but he had to give her credit for having a kind enough heart to make an emotional connection with the dog, despite the fact that such interactions were usually unsuccessful. Nevertheless, that didn't prove her innocence. She'd already admitted having a soft spot where Boyd was concerned. She could have helped him sneak on and off the base at the very least, although Linc couldn't imagine why she would, particularly since she seemed worried about the safety of her little boy.

Truth to tell, Zoe may not have had anything to do with an actual crime or with Boyd's latest victims, other than the fact that they were all connected to Canyon. Two dog trainers, a basic training instructor and a base cook had all died during the previous month and warning notes had been delivered to other potential targets. The trainers and one other, Chief Master Sergeant Clinton Lockwood, were found with red roses the way past victims had been. Boyd could have done all that himself and probably had, particularly if he was actually inside the base's perimeter fence as they suspected.

Which brought Linc's musings back to Zoe Sullivan. She might have helped her half brother gain access if she thought she was doing the right thing and could handle him. There was certainly a stronger possibility for *her* to have given assistance than there was for any of Boyd's former cronies who were still serving at CAFB to do so. They might have supported his illegal activities when he was still enlisted, but those who had stayed on after his discharge and had advanced in rank now had promising careers to consider.

Linc's pondering was interrupted by the arrival of Captain Justin Blackwood, accompanied by a lone evidence technician and base photographer, Staff Sergeant Felicity James. Linc snapped to attention, as did Zoe. Blackwood returned the salute. "As you were."

"I didn't mean for you to bother about this personally, Captain," Linc told the captain.

"I wanted to see the scene for myself." Blackwood was eyeing Zoe as if he expected her to say or do something odd. "Show me what you found."

"It's more what we didn't find." Linc stepped forward with Star, angling so he could also keep an eye on Zoe. "Sergeant Sullivan said the shooting happened here. She insists there must be evidence."

When he pointed at the base of the door, she spoke up. "I was in the back of the building, sir. I couldn't tell exactly how close to the opening the two people were standing, but I could judge left and right. I put the shooting victim a foot left of center with the shooter to the right of that. Any blood spray patterns should be near the bottom edge of the door."

The Captain looked to the tech, who was opening a forensics test kit. "Okay. Colson will run the door up a few feet so you can check the cement apron, too, and Sergeant James can snap a few pictures for the record."

Complying, Linc wished he had thought of that. Normally, he would have, but he had been so sure the Sullivan woman had fabricated her story he'd been lax. That wasn't good, nor was it fair if she was telling the truth.

Which she isn't, he assured himself. He wasn't sure exactly what her motives were. He didn't have to know. All he was supposed to do was follow her in case her murderous brother tried to make contact.

That was a task he relished. Capturing an escaped serial killer was worth working overtime and putting up with a clever woman's tricks. In a way, it was too bad that Sergeant Sullivan was using her superior intelligence and quick mind to thwart the law. Given different circumstances, he would have admired her.

Watching Captain Blackwood oversee the testing of the base of the roll-up door, Zoe felt her confidence waning. Clearly, they weren't finding the clues she had expected.

When the tech straightened, picked up his gear and shook his head, she knew she'd been bested. But by whom? By what? She was positive she'd witnessed a shooting. The chances of such a violent act leaving no trace were slim to none. There had to be something there. There simply had to be.

Unfortunately, she wasn't trained to find it. She was trained to teach basic flying. Period. Frustration brought unshed tears to her eyes, and she fought to remain stoic. "I saw two people. One shot the other. A body fell."

Linc's left brow arched. "You're sticking to that fairy tale?"

"No, I'm sticking to the truth as I know it. There's a big difference."

Although rancor in Colson's expression was evident, he didn't counter. Instead, he turned to his superior and apologized as if the callout was his own error.

"Sorry, Captain. This false alarm was my fault. The subject was out of my sight for a few minutes, so I can't verify anything that took place during that time."

"Well, see that she isn't again, Colson."

"Yes, sir."

The look that the K-9 cop shot her gave Zoe the shivers. She didn't know how her surveillance could get any worse but figured she was about to find out.

She desperately wanted to counter with a statement of her own but managed to hold her tongue. It was doubtful that either man would believe she'd merely been blowing off steam and overreacting in righteous anger regarding the unfair surveillance situation.

Someday, perhaps she'd have a chance to speak her mind, but this was certainly not it. She was already in enough trouble due to her relationship with her nefarious brother, however strained. Considering all the pressure she'd been under lately, there was also a one-in-a-million chance she might have been imagining things. There had been times recently when confusion over minor things had worried her.

If there was a chance that her mind was playing tricks again, her wisest choice would be to let everyone continue to believe she had made up the shooting story as a distraction. Otherwise, someone might deem her unfit—both as an aviation instructor and as Freddy's mother. No way was she going to allow that to happen. Her job was important, yes. She loved her country and was eager to serve. But her little boy was everything.

THREE

"I can call a cab and escort you home," Linc told Zoe after the captain and tech left.

"That won't be necessary."

"You're right. It isn't. But if you're really as upset as you've been acting, it's sensible." He could almost see the wheels turning in her brain before she nodded.

"I'll walk. But I would like the company, just in case. I have to stop at the side door and pick up my groceries."

The change in Sullivan's demeanor bothered him, not because she had stopped arguing but because she seemed so downtrodden. Still, she'd fooled him before, much to his embarrassment, and could easily be acting again. Making comparisons to her criminal brother was natural. Boyd had been charming when it suited him, then he'd changed into a self-serving killer.

Not that Linc believed Zoe was that bad, he assured himself. But it would behoove him to remember she was kin to a serial killer. She and her brother had had the same father, so there was a chance she had inherited whatever genes that made Boyd so dangerous. That judgment wasn't a lot different from their process of choosing likely candidates for K-9 service. The tendencies for action had to be there before training began or efforts for tight control over those instincts might be time wasted.

Ahead of him, Sergeant Sullivan paused to reclaim her grocery totes and started out the door. Linc tensed, wondering if she'd try more evasive tactics and was mildly surprised when she waited for him to clear the exit with Star and fall in beside her.

"You were right," Zoe said with a sigh. "I should have driven. I'm suddenly exhausted." She paused for a heartbeat. "And, no, I'm not asking for that taxi or hinting that I want you to help carry anything while you're on duty."

Linc harrumphed. "It takes a lot out of you to evade the police, huh?"

"Dodging you wasn't the smartest thing I've ever done."

"They why did you do it?"

"Frustration, I guess. I got tired of being treated like a criminal and decided to rebel a little."

"Not a good idea."

She sighed again, this time more loudly. "Yeah. It seemed kind of okay at the time. At least until the shooting."

Pacing her by shortening his strides, Linc remained silent and waited to see if she'd confess more. Instead, she gave him a cynical glance and said, "I really goofed. I liked it better when you and your cohorts were hiding and just shadowing me."

"You may have seen us once or twice, but most of the time we were out of sight."

She laughed.

Linc was not amused. "Are you insinuating you knew we were keeping you under constant surveillance?"

"Absolutely. For one thing, the fact that I was being watched made me edgy, made my senses tingle the way a hare reacts to a hungry coyote." Pausing, she blushed. "Why do you think I started keeping my blinds closed?"

"Because you were hiding something."

"Yeah, my private life."

"We watched the doors for signs of your brother. We weren't peeking in your windows."

"Says who?"

"Says me. You don't have a very high opinion of our Security Forces, do you?"

They had reached Zoe's four-story apartment building. She stopped at the foot of the concrete walkway to answer. "I think the police, both civilian and military, do an amazing job keeping order and tracking down criminals. What I *don't* like is being considered one of the bad guys."

Linc had to admit she had a point. Assuming she was innocent, of course. He nodded in tacit agreement. "I get that. I do. But suppose you were positive a student pilot was unstable. Would you allow him or her to fly or would you wash them out?"

She made a face. "I've washed out more than one."

"Because that's your job as a flight instructor."

"Yes."

"Then bear with me here," Linc said. "Watching you for clues to finding your brother, Boyd, is my job. Even if you haven't been helping him since he escaped from prison, you can't be certain he won't show up looking for you. We know he or someone mimicking him has been on base or we wouldn't have had threats and killings identified by red roses and predictable notes."

He sensed he was getting through to Zoe. "Do you

plan to spend the rest of the afternoon at home, Sergeant Sullivan?"

"Yes. As soon as I send the babysitter home, Freddy and I are going to play a few games."

"All right. I'll go up with you and check the place over."

"Seriously? You want to search my apartment?"

"Unless you refuse permission. If you do, that points to culpability. My CO can always ask for a search warrant."

"I know. Actually, given the morning I've had, I'd almost welcome it. Just don't scare my little boy. Or the babysitter."

"I'll try not to. I was kind of surprised to see who you got to watch him."

"Portia Blackwood, you mean?"

"Yes." Linc had been shocked to see Justin's daughter show up. "Does her father know she's here?"

"I assume so. Captain Blackwood posted a notice asking parents to consider Portia for babysitting to give her something constructive to do now that she's living with him. I called and left a recorded message and she got back to me."

"I can't believe Blackwood gave her permission to sit for you in the first place, considering the possibility of your brother showing up."

"Oh, dear. I didn't think to ask when she called. Maybe she went behind his back." Zoe lowered her voice. "I'm not sure she'll work out anyway. She didn't seem very enthusiastic when she arrived." She shrugged. "Doesn't matter. My Freddy normally spends a lot of his time at the day care and preschool on base and he's perfectly happy there."

"I can't understand why you called Portia in the first place." Following closely, always on alert, Linc climbed the stairs to the second-story apartment with Zoe and Star. "I hear the captain has his hands full with her."

"Well, that's to be expected," Zoe countered. "He wasn't on scene often until Portia's mother passed away." Linc saw her cheeks redden. "Sorry. That sounded too harsh. I shouldn't be gossiping. I don't know the facts firsthand."

"I'm sure my captain did the best he could in a difficult situation."

"I'm sure he did."

Linc noted she had not locked her apartment door and remarked on it. "I'd really be more careful if I were you."

"I usually am. I guess I figured Portia would lock it when I left." She stepped inside and called, "I'm home!"

Linc saw a barefoot child hurrying toward her, arms open wide as if he hadn't seen her in months. The little boy's grin was a mile wide, and his hazel eyes that matched Zoe's twinkled. His hair was curlier and more blond than light brown, but otherwise he was the spitting image of the staff sergeant.

When she dropped her groceries to scoop the toddler up in her arms, Linc was oddly touched. This was a personal side of her he had not noted. The mutual love was so evident, so strong, it seemed to fill the tiny living room.

Zoe kissed Freddy's cheek as he wrapped his pudgy arms around her neck and shouted, "Mama!" Seconds later, he noticed the dog and started to squirm. "A puppy!"

"Whoa. Hold on, honey. That's not a puppy you can

play with. That's a member of the air force, just like Mama is. The dog is working right now."

"That's right," Linc said. "Star and I are going to go check your house while you and your mother wait right here. We'll be back in a few minutes and then I'll introduce you. Okay?"

The eager child was nodding. "Uh-huh."

"Good." Linc looked around. "Where's your baby-sitter, Sergeant Sullivan?"

"Beats me." She turned to her son. "Where's Portia, Freddy?"

"She has time-out."

Zoe was obviously confused. That made two of them. Concerned and on high alert, Linc gave her a hand signal to wait, then took Star and began to work his way through the apartment, room by room. Only one door was closed.

He placed the heel of his hand on the grip of his holstered pistol, prepared to make entry and threw open the door.

Portia's ensuing scream was loud enough to be heard over the roar of a jet engine.

Zoe clasped Freddy tightly and took cover behind the kitchen island. It wasn't until she heard the clicking of Star's nails on the hardwood floor that she raised enough to peek over the top. There was her so-called babysitter, clasping an iPad to her chest and breathing hard. Linc and Star were herding her ahead of them and it was evident she was one unhappy teen.

Rising, still holding her son close, Zoe scowled. "Where did you find her?"

"Sitting on a bed with the door shut, so she could

instant message her friends without being disturbed."
He gave the girl a light tap on the shoulder to urge her
to fully face Zoe and the boy as he continued. "I'm glad
you weren't gone long, Sergeant. If you had been, who
knows what might have happened."

"I agree." Swallowing her anger, Zoe spoke as
sternly as possible while her insides quaked with fear
for Freddy's welfare. "I'm afraid I won't be able to use
your services again, Portia. I'm sorry."

"Whatever." The sullen teen flipped her long blond
hair back defiantly.

"We're both fortunate that the person who scared you
just now is one of the good guys," Zoe said. "It could
have been anyone."

Portia huffed. "Here? We might as well be in jail."

"Normally, I'd agree with you," Zoe said, eyeing
Linc for clues to his opinion of how she handled the
situation and feeling assured they were both on the
same page.

She addressed the girl. "I put aside two hours' wages
for you before I went to the store to make sure I had the
right change." She sat Freddy on the counter and steadied him while she reached up to open the overhead spice
cabinet. "It's right—"

Stunned, Zoe stopped with her hand raised. "I know
I put it here. I remember doing it."

Linc spoke quietly. "Is it possible you only meant to
leave the money and it slipped your mind because you
were distracted?"

"I don't think so." Zoe was beginning to wonder herself, although there was no way she'd admit it, particularly not to him. "All right, Portia," she said, reaching

into her pocket and pulling out a handful of bills. "Here. If this isn't enough, I can write you a check."

The girl grabbed the money without counting it. "I don't need your check. I only took this job in the first place to get out of the house." Still clutching her iPad, she hurried to the door and let it slam behind her.

"Whew." Zoe let out a breath. "I wouldn't want to be that girl's father. It's hard enough being a single parent without stumbling into the job late the way the captain did. It's too bad he wasn't able to be a stronger presence in the girl's life when she was younger."

"Yeah. Deployment can mess up families." Linc eyed the half-open kitchen cabinet and scowled. "You know, you have been under a lot of stress lately."

"Meaning?"

He shrugged. "Maybe it's finally getting to you. You're all by yourself with a child to worry about. You're under suspicion. Your convict brother could show up here at any minute and you still have to perform your normal teaching duties. That's a lot to process."

"Why don't you just spit it out?" Zoe demanded. "You and your boss are sure I imagined the shooting and now you're suggesting I'm losing it over little things, too."

"Are you?"

"No." It was almost a shout and frightened her son into reaching for her. Penitent, Zoe lifted him into her arms and stepped back. "I'm sorry if I scared you, honey." Looking at Star, she asked Linc, "Did you mean it when you promised he could pet your partner?"

"I did." To Zoe's delight, the man even smiled slightly, although it didn't quite reach his eyes.

"Let's go into the living room where we can be comfortable," Linc said, leading the way. "I normally don't take Star's vest off when we're working, but I'll make an exception today." He sat on one end of the small sofa with his K-9 at his feet and proceeded to unbuckle her harness.

"Where should we sit?" Zoe asked, realizing that whatever Colson said, she'd end up close to him. There was no way she was going to get one inch away from her three-year-old son in the presence of a trained attack dog so, like it or not, she was going to have to grit her teeth and cozy up to the security man.

"Right here is fine," he said, keeping his attention focused on Star while indicating the empty end of the settee.

Yup. Really close, she thought. *Oh, well, I can do anything for Freddy's sake. I certainly don't want him to grow up scared of authority or become a criminal like his uncle, Boyd.* Boyd's latest crimes made her almost wish she hadn't taken back her maiden name. Given the treasonous acts associated with her late husband and her plans to make the air force her career however, it had seemed the lesser of two evils. She supposed it still was.

To Zoe's surprise, the cop seemed to mellow as he relaxed and petted the rottweiler. His voice was low, his expression appealing. When he spoke softly to Star, the K-9 gazed into his eyes with total adoration. The pair had gone from imposing threats to friendly neighbors in the blink of an eye. Why couldn't Sergeant Colson act this way when he was shadowing her? She would have liked him a lot better if he had.

That thought stopped her heart. Liked him? Her? No way. He was just another problem to face, another hapless bird sucked into her jet intake, ready to cause a crash. So why was she having such a hard time continuing to dislike him?

Because he was being so kind to Freddy, she answered easily. A big scary cop and a trusting little boy were relating to each other as if they were meant to be best buds.

Linc held out his large hand and Freddy grasped it without hesitation. The sight of the man safely guiding her son's little chubby fingers toward a dog powerful enough to harm them touched her heart. Her son had never known his father, never had a male role model. And until that moment, Zoe had not realized the enormity of what he'd been missing.

FOUR

Linc wasn't surprised by the way Star treated the trusting little boy after a proper introduction, but his own reactions to the situation gave him pause. A feeling of tenderness he had not anticipated flowed over and through him, leaving a sense of peace and rightness behind. What was that all about? He didn't even like kids. At least he didn't think he did. Truthfully, his experiences with small children were limited, and he'd always viewed them as sort of alien creatures. Cute but unknowable. So how had he apparently managed to connect with this one?

He cast a sidelong glance at Zoe and was awed by her expression, as well. The way she was gazing at her son left no doubt of her love and devotion. From what Linc could recall, nobody had ever looked at him that way, not even his own mother, and as far as his dad was concerned, he might as well have been invisible— unless he'd misbehaved. Then his father had taken plenty of notice and dished out serious punishment.

Such thoughts pulled Linc from his earlier calm and left him wondering what Freddy's father had been like. There wasn't much background information in Sergeant Sullivan's personnel file, but since she'd chosen to revert to her maiden name, he figured there must have been notable conflict.

"You're doing fine," Linc told the child. "Just pet her gently. She likes her ears scratched like this." He demonstrated, then laughed when Freddy tried it. "Not so hard, okay? Star wants to keep her ears attached to her head. She needs them to hear with."

Freddy giggled. "Silly."

Linc's grin was genuine and widening. He really got a kick out of this kid. "Here. Let me tell her to lie down and you can scratch her tummy. She loves that, too."

Instead of bending over Star as she dropped to the floor and rolled onto her back on command, Freddy threw himself down beside her and reached across her body to wiggle his fingers in her short soft hair. "Tickle, tickle."

She turned her head without rising and gave his cheek a lick. Childish laughter filled the room, and the boy put his hands over his face. "Eww. She kissed me."

"Because she likes you," Linc replied. He looked at Zoe. "I hope you don't mind."

"It does my heart good to see Freddy so happy. If it takes a little dog slobber to make that happen, how can I mind? Besides, the newest info on keeping kids healthy is to raise them with animals and let them build up resistance to germs."

"Good to know." Linc startled slightly when his radio went off, and he cupped a hand over his earbud, listening to the dispatch coming over his radio.

Zoe gently touched his forearm. "Is everything okay? It's not Boyd, is it?"

"No." Linc put on his blue beret and gave Star's leash a tug. "We have to go downstairs for a few minutes. A couple of our dogs that were still missing after they were all released last month have been sighted coming this way. I'm supposed to keep an eye out and try to capture them."

It was all he could do to avoid looking at the place where her hand still lay. The sensation was electric. When she withdrew her slim fingers, he almost wished she hadn't.

"We won't go far," he said, rising. "Hand me your cell phone and I'll enter my number. We'll be right downstairs if you need anything."

"I can manage my brother if he does show up," Zoe countered, complying anyway. "He doesn't scare me."

"Well, he should." Linc gave her back her phone and paused just long enough to put his dog's working vest back on her. That also gave him time to be certain Zoe was taking his warning seriously. When she sobered, he was satisfied.

Star accompanied him to the door, tight at heel position. Linc glanced back. "Lock this after me."

"I will."

"Now," he added, when she didn't immediately act.

"Yes, sir," she said, giving him a smile and a mock salute.

More chatter was coming in over his radio. Linc keyed his mic. "On my way. I'll meet you in the street."

With a last look at the woman and child, he turned on his heel and left. Normally, he would have waited until he was certain she had locked her door, but the last messages indicated that several of the missing dogs were nearby. His plan was to position himself on the lawn of the apartment building and wait, hoping that Star's presence would draw the others in. Many of the highly skilled K-9s had been found and returned to the CAFB training facility, but there were still thirty-two dogs missing, including four special animals. He wanted to find all the dogs, of course, but locating Glory, Patriot, Scout and Liberty would be a real coup.

A Security Forces SUV was approaching slowly, driver and passenger scanning the area. Linc waved them down.

"I haven't spotted any loose ones yet, but I just got down here," Linc called.

Novice trainer Bobby Stevens, the driver, nodded and glanced up at the apartment windows. "We have an audience. Did they see anything?"

Linc followed the same line of sight and felt his heart skip like a flat stone thrown onto the surface of a placid lake. Zoe and Freddy were peering out their open window, watching the drama in the street unfold.

"No. I was working up there with Star when I got the call. We were all sitting in the living room."

The SUV passenger, Master Sergeant Caleb Streeter, chuckled wryly. "Must be nice getting to sit around all day, Colson, while the rest of us bust a gut chasing reports of dogs."

Under different circumstances, Linc might have returned the taunt. Instead, he chose to tamp down his pride and stay silent. The most important task was catching the Red Rose Killer, and as long as Zoe Sullivan was on base, she was still their best, most important lead.

In the shadowed corners of his mind lurked the realization that he also wanted to keep her safe. Her and her little boy, a child whose openness and charm had touched his heart in a way he couldn't begin to explain. Maybe it was Freddy's lack of a father that made him identify with the boy, Linc mused, remembering the shame his own dad had brought upon him and his mother by going AWOL, becoming a thief and finally being arrested and jailed.

That was one thing he unfortunately had in common with Zoe. Neither of their families was anything to be proud of. And neither of them could do a thing about changing the past. Linc had spent his adult life trying to rise above the stigma of his untrustworthy, unreliable father.

The comparison between his situation and Zoe's struck him like the blast from a jet engine. He was not a bit like his father, so why did everybody seem to think Zoe Sullivan would side with her brother, given the opportunity?

Because she'd kept in such close touch with Boyd, he reasoned, clenching his jaw. That was the difference, and it was a big one.

His eyes were drawn to the apartment window again. As a single mother who had the responsibility of caring for Freddy, would she jeopardize his well-being for the sake of a killer? Approaching the question logically, Linc didn't think so. The trouble was Boyd had always been good at hiding his true nature, at least at first. The women who had refused to date him and men who had somehow crossed him had paid the price for thwarting the emotionally twisted man. Could his seemingly innocent sister be the same kind of person?

A loose German shepherd, tail flagging and ears erect, drew Linc's thoughts back to the current task. The dog was trotting toward Star, panting as if smiling and acting ready to play.

Linc crouched down. "Come here, boy. That's a good boy."

Although the dog slowed and lowered its head as if deciding whether or not to flee, it continued in their direction, then stopped nose to nose with Star. Linc's hand moved slowly, surely, until he was able to slip a looped leash around its neck. The shepherd wore no collar or ID band but since each member of the training project had been microchipped, he knew the dog would easily be identified.

Streeter had left the vehicle, and Linc handed him the dog he'd caught. "Looks like this poor guy missed a few meals. Do you want me to hang around down here a little longer, just in case others show up?"

Streeter shook his head. "No. I'll load this one and cruise the rest of the neighborhood."

"Copy," Linc replied. He didn't particularly like taking orders from a sergeant who was technically not his boss, but it was a reasonable request. Besides, he wasn't eager to return to the Sullivan apartment until he'd figured out why being there had rattled him so.

He'd realized he'd carelessly let down his guard. That was a mistake. A huge mistake. One he would not repeat.

"Look, Mama. Another puppy!" Freddy was peering through the screen as Zoe steadied him.

"I see them. Looks like your friend Star has somebody to play with."

"I wanna go play, too."

"Not now, honey. The policeman is working and so is his dog. We have to stay up here and just watch."

"Aww."

"No whining." Zoe tried to distract him. "How about a game on the iPad? You can make some doggies wag their tails."

"Naw. I wanna watch real puppies. They're soft. I love them."

"Not all dogs are as nice as Star," Zoe warned, "and she might not be fun if Sergeant Colson didn't tell her it was okay. You need to be very careful with all dogs. Ask permission before you try to pet them. Promise?"

Freddy nodded vigorously, but Zoe had doubts he'd take her advice until he was older and wiser. That was the trouble with small children. Until they'd had experience, they were willing to try just about anything. After today, she would have to be doubly vigilant about his interactions with strange animals.

A noise behind her caught Zoe's attention. Frowning, she froze. What was that? It sounded like the squeak in the hallway floor. Listening intently, she didn't hear it repeated. Nevertheless, she started to glance over her shoulder.

Nothing there. She began to feel foolish. *Boy, am I jumpy.* She was turning back to the window when she sensed more than saw movement in her peripheral vision. Instinct made her tighten her hold on her son. Was there actually somebody there?

An instant later, she whirled and put substance to her jitters. A figure in a dark hoodie was tiptoeing across the far end of the small living room!

Zoe thrust Freddy behind her and held him there, hoping and praying she didn't look as scared as she was. With the hoodie masking the side of his face, there was no way to identify the intruder. One thing was certain—he was too slightly built to be Boyd.

"Get out of here," Zoe ordered, relieved that the quaking of her insides wasn't reflected in her voice.

The figure stopped dead. Nobody moved. Zoe could feel the pounding of her pulse in her temples.

A weapon. She needed a weapon. Anything with which to defend her innocent child. But what? The only people on base who were armed were members of the Security Forces and posted guards. Casting about, she saw nothing usable. That left bravado as her only option, and lots of it.

"I said get out of here." It was a commanding order, almost a shout, and Zoe felt her son grasping her legs from behind, the way he did when he was frightened.

A hand with slim but masculine fingers rose to pull the sides of the hood closer. The man dipped his head, averted his gaze momentarily, then pulled something from his pocket.

A knife!

Zoe gasped. Her resolve deepened, hardened, became the wall she needed to protect her little boy. She dropped into a combative stance, feet apart, arms extended and ready to fend off the coming attack. No low-life with a blade was going to get past her. Not if she had anything to say about it.

Freddy had backed off and begun to cry as she'd prepared to do battle. The attacker turned to the boy for an instant, then focused back on Zoe.

She grabbed her jacket off the couch and wrapped it around one forearm, never letting her concentration stray. The man seemed hesitant, as if having trouble choosing his next move. That was to her advantage. She didn't want to face him hand to hand but intended for him to believe she would.

Her mouth was so dry she couldn't swallow, let alone muster a convincing threat. So there they stood as the seconds ticked off, Zoe braced and ready and her adversary hesitating until the hand with the weapon began to visibly shake.

She had him worried. Good. Now all she needed to do was force him to bolt. Would a charge do it? Maybe. And maybe it would trigger his predatory instincts and drive him toward her.

Before she could decide, Freddy touched the back of her leg and whimpered. "Mama?"

Habit caused her to react. She eased her stance momentarily and lowered one outstretched hand toward the boy. That was all the opening her enemy needed. He leaped at her, falling short because she dodged just in time.

With a guttural roar, she charged, coming in low and catching him at the waist the way a football player would take out an opponent.

The man stumbled backward and fell.

Zoe went for the knife and managed to grab his wrist before he threw her off and started to scramble away with his weapon.

She raised the hoodie-wrapped forearm in case he chose to turn and slash at her. Time seemed to slow to a snail's pace. He flipped onto his hands and knees, combat boots slipping on the slick flooring, and crab-walked until he could regain his footing.

Zoe screamed, afraid he was going to detour toward her son.

Freddy was already at the window, waving his hands and yelling, "Help," in his screechy little voice.

The attacker threw the bolt and jerked open the door. Momentum carried him into the hallway.

Breathless, Zoe followed, inhaled as deeply as she could and let loose with a blood-curdling shriek. "Colson! Stop him!"

FIVE

Linc was moving toward the apartment building before he knew what was happening. Star ran ahead of him, barking.

He took the stairs two at a time, reaching the second floor and immediately spotting Zoe braced in her open doorway.

"What's wrong?"

She gestured with her arm. "A man. That way. Down the back stairs. Camo pants and a dark hoodie."

Star was straining at her leash. Linc drew her in and hesitated only long enough to ask Zoe, "Are you okay?"

"Yes! Go! Don't let him get away."

He would have given Star a tracking command if he'd felt it was necessary. In this case, she was clearly on the fresh trail and needed no more encouragement. Had Zoe forgotten to lock her door after him? Worse, could he have overlooked someone hiding in the apartment? He'd checked it thoroughly.

Except for the room where Portia had been, Linc added, berating himself. Careless. Unprofessional at best. He had allowed himself to assume that the teenage girl was alone when she may have had company. She wouldn't be the first babysitter to entertain friends when she should have been minding a child. The instant messaging beeps from her iPad and the absorbed look on her face had thrown him enough that he'd never thought of checking the room further.

But he'd surprised Portia. How would a friend have had time to hide? More important, where was the guy now? Star was still straining at her leash, but there was nobody in sight.

They reached the rear parking area just as a motorbike roared off. Star might have been able to keep up for a short distance if Linc chose to release her, but there was no use endangering the K-9's welfare when he wouldn't be there for the takedown and arrest.

Linc shaded his eyes, trying to make out details of the bike and its rider. But the sun was too bright.

"Star. Out," he commanded forcefully.

Although she remained excited, acting eager to continue her pursuit, she obeyed. Linc knew that his primary task was watching and monitoring the actions of Sergeant Sullivan. Given the state she'd been in as he'd passed her door, he figured it was best to return for an explanation. Assuming she'd offer one.

It bothered him that he still doubted her, yet what choice did he have? She was who she was, the sister of a convicted murderer. Anything beyond that fact was only relevant to where it led them in locating Boyd Sullivan and halting his latest killing spree. Part of him felt sorry for Zoe and her little boy, while another part kept warning him to keep his distance, particularly emotionally. There was no room for sentiment in his job. No place for opinions not based on hard evidence.

And right now, the evidence kept indicating that Sergeant Sullivan was trouble with a capital *T*.

* * *

Zoe had kept watch at her door, just in case. Plus, she wanted to be ready to identify whomever the cop and his dog captured. When she saw them returning alone, her heart fell.

"He got away? How? You had to be right behind him."

"Motorbike," Linc replied. "Star could have kept up on foot for a short distance, but I couldn't have."

"You let him go? Just like that?" Wheeling in a huff, she reentered her apartment and scooped up Freddy, holding him close and murmuring words of comfort.

"What happened anyway? Where did the guy come from?" Linc asked.

"I don't know. I'd locked the door like you told me to, so I guess he was inside all along." Her eyes narrowed on Linc, and she grimaced. "I can't believe you missed him when you checked."

"Neither can I. Stay here a sec while I take a second look."

"Better than the first time, I hope." She knew she was being hypercritical, but someone had just threatened her child and her mother-tiger instincts were still strong.

As soon as Linc and Star returned to the living room, Zoe apologized. "Look. I'm sorry I snapped at you, but that guy was scary. He had a knife."

"What? You didn't tell me that."

"You didn't give me a chance. Besides, I wanted you to hurry up and catch him."

"All right," Linc said, sobering and pulling a small notebook and pen from a deep pocket on his ABU. "Start at the beginning and tell me everything."

By the time she was finished relaying the basics of

her scare, Zoe felt exhausted. She yawned. "Sorry. I guess the rush of adrenaline is wearing off."

"You're not on duty today?"

"No. I had planned to shop, as you already know, then do some housecleaning and relax with Freddy."

"What about tomorrow?"

"We usually go to church on Sunday mornings. If you're still assigned to watch me then, I think you're allowed to bring the dog inside."

"I am. I just don't usually go to church."

"Why not?" Zoe smiled. "Afraid the roof will cave in if you show up?"

"Something like that. I wouldn't want to shock your pastor."

"I think Pastor Harmon will be okay with it. He's a seasoned preacher." Sobering, she added, "I'm starting to appreciate your diligence more than I did before. I really would feel safer if you—or another officer—were with me. With us."

Watching Linc nod, she wondered if the concern she was sensing was real or imaginary. His expression was hard to read when he was at ease. The way he had looked as he and K-9 Star had dashed past her in the hallway, however, was quite memorable. It would be a long time before she forgot his intensity or the way his courageous actions had made her feel. Being married to John Flint had not imparted that kind of cosseted feeling, although belonging to the air force had given her security and a stable place to call home. At least until her brother had been dishonorably discharged, arrested and convicted as a serial killer. Those events had changed everything.

Oh, her job had continued afterward and she'd managed to retain rank, but there had been a subtle shift in the way she was perceived by her fellow airmen. Her troubles had actually begun even earlier when she'd discovered that her late husband had been disclosing details of base operations to unnamed parties. Zoe had taken the proof of it to her superiors immediately. It had been the right thing to do, yet she'd been so mortified she'd almost resigned. If not for the assurances of her officers and thanks from the Department of Homeland Security, she just might have crawled off to lick her wounds and given up the career she loved.

And now Boyd was back.

Yes, she had her son and the best job in the world, but what would keep her brother from spoiling the life she'd hammered out for herself?

Listening to Linc as he reported the incident and requested a tech team to dust for fingerprints, Zoe shivered. Just when she'd thought things couldn't get any worse, they had done just that. As one thing led to another, she felt surrounded by so many unknowns—it was mind-boggling. Being so beset by problems also made her dredge up past failures. Normally, she wasn't so hard on herself, but these current circumstances were enough to cause her to question her choices the way she used to. That not only wasn't good, it wasn't fair to herself or to those around her. Freddy needed a strong, capable parent, not a whimpering, worried mama. She would give him what he needed if it killed her.

In the hidden corners of her subconscious, there lingered the notion that she might be more right than she wanted to be. Her stalker might very well bring death. And then who would look after her son?

Linc left Star sitting with the Sullivans as he welcomed the tech team and their evidence gathering equipment. "There was definitely an uninvited guest in here," he told them. "According to the sergeant, the guy was too slightly built to be Boyd Sullivan, but treat this scene as if it could have been him just the same. No sense taking chances."

The lead tech was the same one who had inspected the warehouse for him. "You sure this time?"

"Sure enough," Linc replied. "He was apparently hiding in the bedroom, and she saw him trying to sneak off. Star and I chased him out the back. He rode away before I got a look at him, but this was no figment of Sullivan's imagination. Star was hot on a trail."

"Gotcha. We'll start in there."

Zoe had been waiting in the background while Linc spoke. He caught her studying him when he turned. The expression on her pretty face didn't suit him, so he approached. "Look, Sergeant, I understand how all this can seem a bit overwhelming but we'll get to the bottom of it eventually."

"Not if people keep insinuating it's all in my head." She sighed. "At least I know your dog believes me."

"I have no doubt you saw somebody."

"*Saw?* I had my hands on him."

"You what?"

"You heard me. When he acted as if he was going to go for Freddy with that knife, I rushed him." She pointed. "We crashed to the floor together right over there. I had hold of his wrist, but he threw me off and ran. I guess I should be thankful he didn't decide to cut me on his way out."

"Stay right there. Don't move. Don't touch anything," Linc ordered. It was only a few strides to the hallway and bedrooms where he called, "One of you get back in here and check for trace evidence. Now!"

His next words were for Zoe. "What else are you withholding?"

"Nothing. I wasn't withholding that." Her hands were clasped in front of her. "Look. I was in combat mode, okay? Details were fuzzy. Some still are. All I know for sure is that I charged him when I thought he was going on the attack."

Linc glanced over at her son. "At least one of you had the presence of mind to call for help."

"Did he? Good for Freddy. That didn't register with me either. Nothing did except the fight I was in. I do remember screaming, probably at you, come to think of it."

"Maybe." Linc shook his head. "You were certainly hollering something when I hit the top of the stairs. Are you always so excitable?"

"Only when somebody is threatening to kill me," Zoe countered. She rolled her eyes. "You don't need to act as if I'm a hysterical female, okay? I'm actually very levelheaded and sensible. Most of the time. I'd have to be to have dealt with the significant others in my life."

"Your brother."

"And my late husband. But that's a story for another time." She stood still as evidence techs inspected her hands and stroked her skin with sterile cotton swabs. "I can't imagine that there's anything there."

"Maybe not," Linc said. "But when there is even a

remote chance of touch DNA, it makes sense to take samples." He addressed the technician. "Check her clothing, too. She says she grappled with the prowler, so there may be something stuck to her body, as well."

"I wish you'd been this thorough in the warehouse," Zoe drawled. "There had to be some kind of evidence there."

"Yeah. From any one of the hundred or so people who had passed through in the last few weeks," Linc countered. "This is different. You and Freddy are the only ones living here. If anything from the attacker rubbed off on you, we'll detect it."

"Who do you think it was?" she asked.

"Well, I'm beginning to doubt it was your brother if that's what you're asking," Linc said. "Knowing that he pulled a knife on you and you tackled him changes everything. If it had been Boyd, I imagine you'd have tried to talk him down." It amused him to see her rolling those warm hazel eyes again, and he chuckled softly. "Hey, I just tell it like it is."

"No," Zoe countered, "you tell it like you think it is. There's a huge difference."

He decided to humor her now that the techs had stowed their samples and returned to the bedroom where the man had probably been hiding. "Okay. Here's what I think happened. You hired Portia to babysit, and she invited a young man to keep her company. When he heard you come home, he probably thought you were alone and he hid. Then, when I checked the bedroom and rousted Portia, I failed to let Star search the rest of the room. That's on me."

"You think he was here all that time?"

"Yes, unless you left your back door open."

"Never. There's a dead bolt and chain on it so Freddy won't wander out on to the deck."

Linc shrugged and spread his hands. "There you have it. You probably scared that guy so badly he'll never come around again." To his relief, Zoe began to smile.

"I sure hope so. He scared me plenty."

"Are you okay now?" Although he expected her to affirm her well-being, he hadn't imagined she would be so candid.

"Yes," Zoe said, her smile softening. "I'm okay. You're here."

She averted her gaze, but not before Linc noted the glistening of unshed tears and felt his gut clench in empathy.

SIX

"I don't care what some anonymous blogger wrote. There's no way Zoe Sullivan faked a prowler to try to distract us from the search for her brother," Linc told Captain Justin Blackwood. "For one thing, I saw a guy fleeing." They and others were gathered in the Security Forces headquarters for a meeting of the team assigned to bring down Boyd Sullivan. Besides the regular air force members, there was Oliver Davison of the FBI and Special Agent Ian Steffen from the Office of Special Investigations.

Blackwood nodded. "All right. We'll go with that conclusion. I've talked to my daughter about the incident, and she's denied having anyone in the Sullivan apartment with her, but I've done enough interrogating to suspect she may be lying." He shook his head slowly. "Makes me wish I hadn't deployed so often when she was growing up. I hardly know her."

"We can't go back," Master Sergeant Westley James chimed in. "If we could, I'd save the lives of my two murdered team members." He cleared his throat. "Of course, I did end up marrying Felicity after successfully protecting her, so some good did come out of the Sullivan incursion."

"True." Blackwood addressed the group. "Any other

leads on our escaped felon? I want to hear your ideas even if you don't think they're relevant." He was quite serious when he added, "Remember, besides the murders, Boyd Sullivan's the reason we're still missing so many valuable K-9s."

Special Agent Davison spoke up. "Some of my people participated in a ground search for your dogs, as you know. Senior Airman Ava Esposito helped organize the grid and worked with her search-and-rescue K-9, Roscoe. One of the others said he was the survivor of a chopper crash."

Linc nodded. "Probably Senior Airman Isaac Goddard. He's trying to bring a heroic German shepherd home from Afghanistan and adopt him, so I know he has a heart for dogs."

"Anything else?" Blackwood asked, scanning his team in the conference room.

Linc cleared his throat. "Well, sir, it's not directly related to the missing dogs, but there is something odd Sergeant Sullivan said recently. I checked her file again and didn't find much about John Flint, her late husband. What's the deal on him? Could he have had any connection to her brother?"

Hesitating long enough to make Linc uneasy, the captain said, "Some of her personal information has been redacted. It's my understanding it was done as a reward for actions she took on behalf of Homeland Security, but there's no way I can access their sealed files. If you want to know more, I suggest you ask her directly."

"Do you think she'll tell me?"

"If you get closer to her, she might," Sergeant James

interjected. "I hear she's already beginning to rely on you and Star. That's good."

Uncomfortable with the direction the conversation was taking, Linc cleared his throat. "Are you ordering me to make this personal?"

"I can't do that, Sergeant. But I can tell you it's important that we put an end to the Red Rose Killer's actions both on and off the base. If Zoe Sullivan holds the key to doing that, I expect you to take every advantage offered, even if it means sacrificing some personal comfort."

"She seems good at heart," Linc argued.

"Then it won't hurt you to befriend her, will it? I'll make it easy for you. Except for required days off, she'll be your only assignment. Make the most of it. Since you two already seem to have a slight bond, I'm going to rotate your relief so she concentrates more on you. The new duty schedule will be posted this afternoon."

"Yes, Master Sergeant. I'll do my best."

And he would. Linc wasn't thrilled with the suggestion that he pretend to become personally involved with Zoe and her son; he was simply resigned to the need for it. As assignments went, it wasn't bad as long as he kept a tight grip on his feelings and guarded his heart well enough. He'd do it for the air force, for his country. The way he viewed it, he wouldn't be doing anything wrong as long as he didn't lead Zoe on or let her believe he was romantically interested in her.

The trick was going to be convincing himself that subterfuge was a necessity and that he wasn't becoming the kind of lowlife his father had been. He'd spent most of his adult life living down that odious man's sins, and any inkling that his own honor might be at risk gave him a sense of foreboding. Linc knew he was as human as anyone, but he had long ago vowed that he would never display even the slightest hint of dishonesty. He would not follow in his thieving, lying father's footsteps. Ever. Neither would his loyalty ever come into question. Not if maintaining it literally killed him.

Zoe had Freddy up and dressed for Sunday services in plenty of time. She had seen a dark-colored SUV parked in the street below her apartment and assumed it belonged to the Security Forces. Was Linc in it? Part of her yearned to see him again, while another part of her worried that she might be starting to get too dependent upon him—and his K-9 partner.

Freddy had no such qualms. "Is the doggy going to church with us?" he asked, bouncing on his tiptoes with excitement.

"I don't know, honey. It's possible."

"You asked. I heard. So he's going, right?"

Zoe had to smile at the child's expectations of the perfect day. "The Security Forces man may bring Star if they're on duty today. We'll have to wait and see."

"They could come anyway."

"I know. I know." But the chances of that were probably slim, she added to herself. No telling why Linc had acted so put off when she'd suggested he accompany them to church, but she didn't think it had anything to do with her or Freddy. No, it was something else. Something deeper. He wouldn't be the first soldier to turn from God after experiencing combat, although oftentimes the reverse was true. Strong Christians could be formed in the trenches, too. It all depended on the man or woman and their willingness to trust in a higher power rather than relying only upon themselves. Bowing a knee could be tough for someone who had always felt totally self-reliant.

Or for someone who simply chose evil over good, as her brother had. Sadly, she was beginning to lose hope that Boyd would ever repent. At this point, the most she could hope for was that he'd stop hurting others and be brought to justice. As much as she'd loved the boy he'd been when they were growing up, she could not accept his adult self. Whatever goodness was still inside him had been masked by a blackness that encompassed his heart and made him a different person. Someone who had to be stopped. In that regard, she almost wished he would contact her, because she wouldn't hesitate to turn him in.

A small head ducked beneath her hand and she felt Freddy's silky hair. "Don't be sad, Mommy. If the doggy doesn't come, you can pet me. See?"

Laughing, Zoe gave his hair a gentle tousle. "Okay. But you have to promise to behave in church and not bark."

The child's eager "Ruff, ruff" made her chuckle more.

"Careful or you'll be eating kibble instead of cookies."

He giggled, eyes sparkling. "I'm not really a dog. Little boys need cookies."

"Okay." She smoothed the skirt of her dress and patted her knot of hair that she'd twisted neatly and clipped at her nape. "You ready?"

"Uh-huh." Freddy grasped her hand.

"Then let's go."

The closer Zoe got to the street, the more butterflies

there were cavorting in her stomach. Would Linc be waiting? Would he go to church with them? She kept telling herself he wouldn't, but in the back of her mind was the hope he would. Why it mattered, she wasn't sure, but she desperately wanted him with her. Going to services was a step in the right direction, and perhaps she was meant to be the catalyst that led him back to the fold.

Yeah, right. Some Christian disciple I am when all I can think about is how safe he will make me feel, she countered. That was the basic truth. She wanted Linc and Star with her for protection far more than for altruistic reasons, and it was just as well to admit it. Matter of fact, she was going to tell him the same thing the first chance she got.

Which was about to be…later, Zoe realized as an unfamiliar enlisted man got out of the SUV and greeted her.

"Good morning, Sergeant Sullivan," the younger airman said with a broad grin. He gestured at the car. "I'm here to give you a ride to church."

"No, thanks. We usually walk."

He sobered. Seemed nervous. "Sorry. I was told to drive you, and if you don't want me to get busted, I'd appreciate it if you'd get in."

Zoe noted that his neck and face had reddened and he was breaking a sweat. "Who did you say sent you?"

"Um, Tech Sergeant Colson."

"I see. You have written orders then?"

"No, ma'am. It's just a *ride*."

If the young airman hadn't sounded so unsure and acted jittery, she might have got into the car without question. Looking around her, Zoe noted others pass-

ing by on the sidewalk and in the street. At least she
and Freddy weren't isolated there. Once she entered the
vehicle, she'd be hidden behind its tinted windows and
lose any advantage she had now.

Despite the fact that the driver opened the rear passenger door for her, Zoe didn't get in. Instead, she
slowly backed away. Her eyes narrowed, taking in everything about the airman and committing his features
to memory. The trouble was, he looked a lot like every
other immature green recruit. Acted it, too.

"You'll—you'll be late for church," he said with a
wheedling tone.

"If I am, I am." Still balancing Freddy on her hip,
Zoe took her cell phone out of her purse and quickly
found the number Linc had entered the day she'd chased
away the prowler. In seconds she had him on the line.

"Colson."

"This is Zoe Sullivan. I want to thank you for sending a car for me, but it's really not necessary."

"What did you say?" His shout was loud enough that
she eased the phone away from her ear. By the time Linc
added, "I didn't send anybody to get you," his words
were practically broadcast volume.

Zoe saw the driver's face pale. "It—it was just…"
he began before wheeling, jumping into the car and
hitting the gas. The tires slipped and screeched on the
pavement. Holding her son close, Zoe stepped up on
the curb and melted into a small crowd of onlookers.

Her phone was still on, Linc's voice strident. "Where
are you now?"

"The street in front of my apartment. He drove off. I
don't know who he was. He said you sent him and I—"

"Stay there. I'm on my way," Linc ordered. She heard

the roar of a motor in the background as he added, "ETA less than five. Are you and the boy all right?"

"We're fine. I didn't fall for the trick."

"Can you ID the vehicle or the driver?"

"It looked like one of your black SUVs. The driver was just a nervous kid."

"The same one you caught in your apartment?"

"I don't think so. This guy was shorter. And less belligerent." She pulled Freddy closer and backed farther from the curb until she was partially standing behind the trunk of one of the cottonwoods lining the street. "How much longer before you get to me?"

"You should be able to hear my siren. I'm only a couple blocks away, turning off Canyon Drive and passing the Base Command Office."

"Copy. We'll wait right here."

As the wailing of Linc's siren grew louder, Zoe's fear waned. She had thwarted an enemy once again, and her knight in shining armor was about to ride up on his prancing steed and protect her.

On second thought, she didn't need any knight. She needed information, some of which her so-called *knight* might be withholding, she realized, because he didn't trust her. Maybe now he'd open up more. As long as she was even partially in the dark about what was going on behind the scenes, she was more vulnerable.

A chill chased up her spine as she thought about their near abduction. Only common sense and a niggling warning in her subconscious had kept her from believing the clean-cut young airman and getting into that car. How many other traps were waiting? How many more dangers would she have to identify and avoid before this nightmare was over?

A black SUV that was the twin of the first one rounded the corner on to her block and skidded to a halt, its siren winding down like a balloon losing air. Zoe had no doubt who was behind the wheel of this one. The sight of Linc Colson leaping out and releasing his K-9 from the rear brought immense relief. It also brought unshed tears to her eyes, tears that were quite embarrassing.

She blinked them away before Linc got close enough to notice. Smiling, she looked up at him. "You made good time. Where were you?"

"Waiting at the church. What happened to your assigned guard?"

"Beats me." She shrugged. "At first, I thought it was the kid who said he was here to pick me up. But when he got out, I could tell he wasn't part of the security team."

"Who was he?"

"I've never noticed him before. This is a big base. I could have walked right past him—and a hundred just like him."

"I have my people looking into it," Linc said. "Part of this is my fault. I thought your night guard would escort you as far as the church. He said when he saw the car pull over and park, he assumed I was picking you up and he left. That kind of mix-up won't happen again."

"I certainly hope not." Zoe spoke from the heart. "I suspect the problem is that you people aren't watching me for my sake. You're here because you expect Boyd to show up."

"Granted. That doesn't mean I'm going to take your reports of trouble lightly."

"Honest?"

"Honest," Linc promised. "If we manage to apprehend the airman who was here this morning, will you be able to ID him?"

"Yes. As soon as he began acting suspicious, I paid special attention to his face. Trouble is, I couldn't read his name tag and he resembles half the guys on base. How did he manage to get the keys to one of your SUVs?"

"That's another very good question."

Zoe sighed as she helped Freddy into the rear seat of Linc's vehicle and, in the absence of a car seat, fastened his seat belt. "In retrospect, this guy seemed more scared than menacing, as if he knew he was in the wrong and didn't want to be there."

"Interesting. Do you think your brother would be capable of fooling a clueless recruit into doing his bidding?"

"My brother again? Why do you keep blaming everything on Boyd? I mean, if he wanted to talk to me, he could just call."

"On the burner phone you smuggled to him in prison?"

Astounded, Zoe gaped at him. "What are you implying?"

"Master Sergeant James and I paid a visit to the prison and spoke with a cell mate of your brother's. He told us Boyd had a burner phone in his possession before his escape."

She stood tall, shoulders back, chin up, and faced him. "Well, he didn't get it from me."

Noting Linc's sigh, she wondered if she might be

getting through to him. He did nod. "Okay. Then where do you think it came from?"

"How should I know? You're the security guy. Was I the only one who visited the prison?"

To her relief, Linc shook his head. "No. One of our aircraft mechanics was there, too. Jim Ahern."

"I think my brother had mentioned him before."

"He may have. They were buddies before Boyd was dishonorably discharged."

"Then why all the interest in me? Why don't you put a watch on Ahern, too?"

"We're not ignoring that possibility," Linc said. He started to reach for the front door on the passenger side. Zoe stopped him. "I'll ride in the back with Freddy, if you don't mind."

Although Linc easily acquiesced, she could tell he wasn't thrilled that she'd refused to sit next to him. Well, too bad. Every time she began to think he might be on her side, he came up with another accusation and proved the opposite.

When Zoe admitted to herself that she wished he wasn't going to church with them, her conscience reared up and gave her a swift kick. Just because somebody was a thorn in her side, that didn't mean that person didn't need the Lord. Maybe Linc was more in need of God's mercy than she was.

Her glance caught his in the rearview mirror, and she was surprised to sense actual concern. Long after he broke eye contact, she continued to observe him. Analyze him. Admire him, despite his contrariness. There was something about the sergeant that impressed her in a way she didn't understand. Moments ago, she'd been wishing he wasn't there, yet now his presence was giving a lift to her spirits and bringing peace to her heart.

That was crazy.

It was also patently true.

SEVEN

Seated in the last church pew with his charges, Linc was fine as long as he kept his focus on doing his job, which meant not allowing himself to relax and enjoy Zoe's or Freddy's company. Star, on the other hand, was having no such qualms and was leaning against the boy's tennis shoes, panting.

The K-9 didn't have Linc's background to create bias. Lies had cost him the lives of men in his former unit, something he would never be able to forget, and more lies threaded through his memories of his father. The parent he'd believed to be a hero had turned out to be nothing more than a thief and a coward, a familial sin he was still doing penance for in his own way.

His father was a lot like Boyd Sullivan, he thought. Slick on the outside and rotten to the core. It wasn't until Zoe nudged him and asked, "Did you have dill pickles or lemons for breakfast?" that he realized his disturbing thoughts were being revealed in his expression.

"I feel as though I've been making a steady diet of sour lemons," Linc replied, "in the form of unanswered questions and out-and-out lies."

"Not to mention the stuff that's been happening to me while you've been assigned to watch me."

Linc saw a scowl beginning to knit her forehead

beneath her bangs, so he continued. "It's all part of the same package. If—and that's a big if—you happen to be telling me the whole truth, we have more than one problem to solve."

"Duh. You think?"

A hush was coming over the congregation. Linc laid his index finger across his lips. "Shush. We'll talk about this later."

"Guaranteed," Zoe said. As the congregation rose, she pulled a hymnal out of the rack on the back of the pew in front of them and expertly thumbed to the called-for page.

Linc did not intend to sing along. He hadn't been in a church since the deaths of some of his best friends and he was far from comfortable. Nevertheless, the music tugged at his boyhood memories of standing in a worship service beside his mother and following her lead as she gave voice to her strong faith. In that respect, Zoe kind of reminded him of his mom. Her pitch was perfect, her tone both soothing and inspiring.

When she extended one side of the open hymnal toward him, he grasped the edge and made a small effort to join in. The more he sang, the more poignant the song seemed. For some reason, words that were familiar suddenly took on deeper meaning, each phrase drawing him closer to the faith he'd once professed.

Linc resisted the inner call. He continued to sing until a catch in his throat made his voice crack. Keeping his eyes forward, he released the hymnal to Zoe and stood at attention. He was a soldier. A member of the elite Security Forces. His own man and afraid of nothing. He didn't need the crutch of religion. He didn't need anything or anybody except his badge and his dog.

As positive as those thoughts were, they weren't enough to banish the tightness in his throat or the sense that he was missing something vital. Something that was almost within his grasp.

Zoe usually felt at home in church, though she might not be at ease in any other group. Even her personal friends had acted rather distant since they'd learned who her brother was and what had been occurring ostensibly because of him. Although she would have liked to come up with a reason to deny some of the charges against her sibling, she knew without a doubt that he was capable of killing on a mere whim. He'd proved it to judge and jury. As much as she wished she could, there was no way to convince herself he might be innocent this time, either.

She had some fond memories of her big brother looking after her when they were children growing up in Dill, Texas. She'd idolized him, following him everywhere when she was a little girl, but current events were undeniable. Boyd had not only confessed in court, he'd acted proud of his crimes and justified for committing them. Therefore, she had no rebuttal for those who blamed Boyd for the terrible things occurring since his escape. He was intelligent yet behaved in a way she couldn't fathom, couldn't identify with. The youth who had stood up for her against playground bullies had chosen to become an abusive adult rather than continuing to champion those who needed help. If he had stayed on the side of law and order, he would have made an excellent military officer or policeman.

As for the personal problems she was currently facing, however, Zoe doubted Boyd would bother to create that kind of chaos. Not only was it unlikely that he'd have known she'd duck into the warehouse in time to see that supposed shooting, he wouldn't have sent an enlisted man to do his bidding that morning when he could easily have contacted her himself. Not to mention whoever had been lurking in her apartment, particularly since Portia had vowed she knew nothing about the prowler and had convinced everybody she was not responsible. That made the whole scenario much, much more terrifying.

Zoe's thoughts were cut short when the service ended. Everyone stood. Zoe let Freddy climb up on the bench beside her, so he'd be at eye level and she turned to speak to Linc. "We usually go out for lunch on Sunday after church. Is that all right?"

"You don't have to ask me," he said flatly. "If you aren't too worried about being out in public, then go."

"I'd almost rather be out and about than back in my apartment, wondering who else is hiding there, ready to pounce. How about the Winged Java for lunch? You're coming with us, right?"

"Absolutely. I have the day duty. Let's get back to the car so I can check my messages in private. I want to see if they managed to nab your SUV driver."

She shuddered. "He's not *mine*. In fact, I hope I never run into him again." Falling into step with Freddy propped on her hip, she said, "By the way, I keep imagining I'm catching glimpses of the shooter from the warehouse. I know it has to be impossible to tell, because his face was covered, but... I don't know. I keep seeing guys who move the way he did, and it gives me the jitters."

"What about his supposed victim? Any sightings of her?"

"No. That actually should be easier because she had reddish hair, but I haven't noticed anybody who looks like her."

"Any more thoughts about the guy in your apartment?"

"I'm just glad he didn't show himself sooner and hurt Freddy," Zoe replied. "Or Portia. Now that I think about it, he probably wasn't one of our airmen. His face was shadowed by the hoodie but it looked grubby, as though he might be growing a beard. Airmen are always neat and their uniforms make them look so handsome."

"You in the market for another husband?"

Cheeks warming, Zoe shook her head. "No way. I've had my fill of smooth talkers and romance. Been there, done that, have the T-shirt and the scars to prove it."

"You mentioned your late husband before. What was the deal with him anyway? I can't find much on file. That is, if you don't mind talking about him."

They had reached the SUV and Zoe had helped Freddy get settled before climbing into the front seat. Linc had briefly checked his messages, then pulled into traffic and was heading for the café before she chose to answer.

"His name was John. John Flint. We met in basic and by the time we were both E-2s, we'd fallen in love and decided to get married."

"I figured out that much. What happened to him? I was told he died in an auto accident, but there are no details on file and all I could find for a cause of death is *unknown*. Did he die of his injuries?"

Hesitating, Zoe studied Linc's profile. As much as

she wanted to deny it, there was something about him that inspired confidence. As long as she didn't reveal the specifics of John's crimes, she supposed it wouldn't hurt to clue him in a little.

"There are questions, suspicions surrounding the accident," Zoe said, keeping her voice soft so Freddy wouldn't overhear. "Officially, the accident caused his death. The reasons behind that crash are something else. I inadvertently unearthed evidence that my late husband had committed crimes and I turned in the evidence. The authorities began to speculate that perhaps he had been…terminated after that, because he knew too much and his usefulness had ended."

"Usefulness to whom?"

"Good question. If they ever did figure it out, I wasn't told."

"Who are *they*?"

"The case eventually made its way to Homeland Security. They're the ones who sealed the files." She noted Linc's scowl and the way his fists gripped the steering wheel. Little wonder. Mention Homeland Security and walls shot up. That agency was the be-all and end-all of national defense. The very fact that it had become involved marked John's death as the act of subversives. Or worse.

"What did you find that implicated him?"

"They asked me not to divulge those details," Zoe explained. "I'm not sure what investigations grew out of the info they got from his laptop, but it no longer matters. John may not have directly murdered innocent people the way my brother has, but he was not the kind of man I thought he was when I married him. If he hadn't died, I'd probably have divorced him when I learned what he'd been up to."

"Could any of that background be influencing what's happened to you lately?"

"I can't see how. It's been years." Sighing deeply, she leaned against the seat. Bothered by the knot of hair at her nape, she pulled the pins that held it in place. Shaking out her tresses, she raked her fingers through them. Linc was watching her out of the corner of his right eye and that much intensity made her nervous. "What?"

Color rose to infuse his cheeks. "Nothing."

"You may as well say it," Zoe grumbled. "Boyd and Freddy's daddy—the men in my life. I can really pick 'em, huh?"

"You didn't pick your brother. He came as part of the family package. My lineage isn't much better."

"Really?"

"Really. Listen, if I tell you something in confidence, will you promise to keep it to yourself?"

"You'd trust me that far?" Her eyebrows arched theatrically. "Maybe you'd better not confess anything. I don't want to be responsible if your deep dark secret gets out."

"It's not about me. It's about my dad. He was in the air force, too, only his record was far from honorable. They caught him stealing and drummed him out of the service. After that, his personal life fell apart and he left my mother. She raised me alone." He leaned his head back, gesturing toward the back seat. "Kind of like you and Freddy."

"Is that why you seem to understand him so well?"

"I don't know. Maybe. What I'm trying to say is, don't beat yourself up about your past. We all make mistakes. It's part of life. The good news is we can turn it around and make amends, because you and I are still alive and kicking."

What was he alluding to? Did he think his speech about his father was going to loosen her tongue? Sure sounded like it. She steeled her nerves and cleared her throat. "Listen, Colson, I went to my commanding officers and did all I could to make things right after John died. And I would do the same now if I had any clues about Boyd. Is that clear?"

"Crystal." Linc slowed as they passed the distinctive Winged Java café with its white coffee mug mural and lit red, white and blue decorative wings. There was a line of customers out front waiting for a chance to enter. "We'll starve before we get a booth in there. What do you say we pick up a pizza from Carmen's instead and eat it back at your place?"

Zoe wanted to argue. She really did. But his suggestion made perfect sense, and she knew Freddy had to be hungry, even if her own stomach was too crowded with butterflies and angst to leave room for food. "Fine. I was going to invite you in, anyway. It looks as if this afternoon is going to be a hot one, and I see no reason to make that poor dog suffer in the heat."

"Can I come in with her?"

Zoe huffed and nodded. "Yes, as long as you behave. No jumping on the furniture—or jumping to conclusions."

"Promise. And maybe if we go back over the recent incidents involving you, we can find some kind of pattern. It's worth a try."

"I've been over and over it. There are no logical connecting factors."

"Only because we haven't discovered them yet," he argued.

"It's not my brother," Zoe told him flatly. "Boyd may be a lot of things but subtle isn't one of them. If he wanted to punish me, he'd come right out and do it. No. Whoever's been messing with me is someone other than him." She lowered her voice. "I'm actually more afraid of the unknown than I am of Boyd. I keep remembering the man in my apartment who pulled the knife on us."

Linc wheeled into the drive-through lane under a red-and-white awning outside Carmen's Italian Restaurant. "Funny you should see it that way," he said. "The same possibilities occurred to me."

She couldn't suppress a relieved smile. "Hooray. Finally. Now we're getting somewhere." The reserved look on his handsome face told her Linc had not come as far in his reasoning as she had. That was okay. At least he'd made a baby step in the right direction.

And for now we're reasonably safe, she added, swiveling to grin at her cute little boy. Being committed to the air force meant she wasn't free to go on the run from her enemies, nor was there any place on the base where she could hide. Not for very long at any rate. That meant standing her ground and bravely facing all foes just as the military she honored did, at home and around the globe.

It might sound clichéd to outsiders, but she was a part of the best fighting force in the world and proud of it. So was the man who sat beside her and imparted both courage and strength. Linc Colson may not feel that close to her as a person, but she was ready to stand by his side against anyone and anything. What she could not accomplish on her own was more than possible with his support. They would succeed and get to the bottom of all that had been happening. Together.

Full realization hit her like a rocket ignition. Zoe's pulse sped, pounding until she wondered if the beats were audible. She had just mentally joined herself to Linc Colson in a way that surpassed anything in her past. The sense that they were already a functioning couple, standing as one, was so strong it left her breathless.

Her first instinct was to deny those conclusions and banish any notions of partnership. But she didn't. She couldn't. Like it or not, she wanted him beside her, now and for as long as unknown foes kept coming at her. So far, they had found no victim of the shooting she'd seen. The person in her apartment had escaped. And she had thwarted this morning's effort to coax her into the wrong vehicle. So far, so good, but how long could that last? Considered together, those instances were enough to set her on edge and keep her looking over her shoulder all the time. Plus, there was the question of the whereabouts of her murderous sibling. Every day brought more angst and increased her fear. Only one element brought relief, and she was most grateful.

Thank You, Lord, for sending Linc and his K-9 into my life, Zoe prayed silently. *I don't care why they're here. I'm just thankful they are.*

EIGHT

It didn't take long to get to the Sullivan apartment with their food. Linc let Zoe handle the pizza box and shepherd her child while he and Star took point. The K-9 began straining at her leash as soon as they reached Zoe's second-story apartment.

"Whoa. Wait," Linc ordered sternly. "I thought I'd convinced you to lock up."

"I did." She leaned to peer past him.

"Well, the door's not even closed all the way, so something happened."

His outstretched hand became a barrier. "You stay out here with the boy while I check inside."

To his dismay, Zoe disagreed. "How do you know this isn't a ploy to get you to leave us alone out here in the hallway so we're vulnerable?"

"That is a valid point," he said. "Okay. Slip inside after I give you the okay and do your best to secure this door. It doesn't look like it's been jimmied so the lock should still work."

"How could—"

"I don't know. One thing at a time, okay? I'm going to make an entry and let Star tell me if there's anybody in here who doesn't belong. I'll leave the door open and signal you to follow as soon as I'm sure it's safer in than out."

Satisfied by her nod, Linc gave the door a push, stood aside with the K-9 and called out, "Security. Anybody in here?"

Star seemed relaxed enough that Linc quickly motioned to Zoe and Freddy to follow him in. They stopped as ordered and waited. The little boy was behaving with extraordinary restraint, probably because he was picking up vibes from the adults.

Linc once again made a barrier with his outstretched arm to keep his charges in place. "Stay here and look around the room. Does anything look different or missing?"

"I think the sofa was moved. It looks farther to the right than I left it. But why would anybody move furniture?"

"Maybe you did it while you were cleaning and forgot."

"Sounds like my whole life lately. My possessions seem to have a mind of their own. I put my purse on one table and it ends up somewhere else when I look for it. Stuff like that."

"Do you think you're just rattled because you're worried?"

"It's possible." She shivered and pressed her back to the closed door while Freddy hugged her knees.

"We'll talk about all that later." Linc gave Star the command "Get 'em" and let her leash extend.

Nose to the floor, the K-9 began to sniff. She coursed back and forth in the living room a few times but surprisingly she alerted on nothing, then proceeded to the kitchenette and then down the only hallway. A few minutes later, she was heading back to the entry.

Linc gave Zoe a shrug and a slight smile as he followed his dog back through the living room. "Nothing positive. Not even a stray prowler."

"Not funny," she said, making a face. "The last time took ten years off my life."

"You can spare them." He unleashed his dog, relieved Zoe of the pizza box and strode toward the small kitchen. "If I hadn't seen your file, I'd have thought you were still a teenager."

"There are times when I feel twice my twenty-six years," Zoe replied. "How old are you?"

"Four, in dog years, if you count them the old way. There's a new complicated formula that's supposed to be more accurate but seven to one is a lot easier."

"Hmm, twenty-eight. I'd have guessed you were older. Sorry."

He had placed the box on her kitchen counter and was washing his hands at the sink. "Not a problem. Looking more mature helps in my job. Besides, there are plenty of miles on me."

"Hard ones?"

Zoe was sponging off Freddy's hands and prepping him for a messy meal, so she wasn't watching Linc when she'd posed the question. He was glad. For an instant, he suspected his face had displayed some of the latent pain and grief he still carried. He'd told her about his father, which was more than she needed to know. He did not intend to brief her on the loss of his human friends or the subterfuge that had cost them their lives.

"Relatively hard," Linc said, working to keep his

tone casual. "I did a tour overseas before coming back stateside and joining Security Forces."

"Did you work dogs over there?"

He shook his head. "No, but their training impressed all of us. That's why I applied to become a handler myself when I came home."

"You seem to be a natural," Zoe told him as she lifted Freddy into his booster seat at the small table. "I used to have a dog when I was little."

Seeing her smile fade and hearing a telling sigh, Linc waited until she'd got drinks for all three of them and was seated before he sat down and continued that line of conversation. "My dad would never let me have a dog, so I mostly hung out with the ones in the neighborhood. Even when they disobeyed their owners, they usually listened to my commands. Labs were my favorite. What breed did you have?"

"Trixie was just a little white mutt, but I loved her," Zoe said without looking at Linc. Her somber mood caused him to reach out. She permitted him to lay his hand over hers where it rested on the table next to her paper plate, and he could feel a slight tremor. "She disappeared."

"You never found her? I'm sorry."

Although Zoe raised her chin and squared her shoulders, he could tell it was an effort for her. When she said, "I think my brother got rid of her because he was mad at me," Linc was dumbstruck. His fingers tightened around hers and Zoe squeezed back. What could he possibly say to help her heal from a trauma like that? A child losing a beloved pet was bad enough. Suspecting that her own brother was behind it had to ache all the way to her core.

Linc placed his other hand over their joined ones and simply waited. This was a truly amazing woman. She had been hurt and had suffered loss repeatedly, yet she'd insisted that there was something inside Boyd worth saving. Was that forgiveness or naïveté? Maybe it was both. And maybe she was relying on her Christian faith for the strength to not only face each day but to soothe the wounds of the past.

He had been counseled to do the same. He knew it would help him cope. But he wasn't ready to forgive the lies that had led to the loss of his friends in combat or the woman who had told them so convincingly. And that didn't include his father's betrayal of their family and the bevy of falsehoods that man had spewed.

Zoe was a better Christian than he'd ever be, Linc ultimately concluded, meaning she was probably telling the truth about Boyd, too. The main reason he hated to admit that was because it meant he was further from apprehending the escapee than anyone had anticipated.

And more innocents were probably going to die.

Staring at their joined hands, Linc promised himself he would not let one of those victims be Zoe Sullivan.

During most of the meal, Zoe had concentrated on Freddy rather than pretending to be upbeat. She did manage to eat a little, but her appetite was nil. Neither she nor Linc had talked a lot, although he had made a few attempts at casual conversation. Freddy, on the other hand, was his usual loquacious self.

"Don't try to talk until you swallow, honey," she prompted. "It's not polite."

"Mmm." His grin would have been edged with tomato sauce if she hadn't been wiping his face frequently as he ate. "When can I play with the puppy?"

"After we're done," she said. "And no feeding her from the table. Dogs don't like pizza."

"Yes they do." To prove his point, the boy leaned to one side and let Star lick his messy fingers.

Linc stopped him firmly. "Don't. Please. Working K-9s are not supposed to take food from anybody but their handlers. You need to help her keep the rules, okay?"

"Okay." Subdued, Freddy straightened while Zoe cleaned the hand that had been offered to Star. "I'm done. Can I play now?"

"After we wash you with soap at the sink," his mother said.

Linc stood first. "I'll take care of him for you. Finish your meal. You've hardly eaten a thing."

She didn't argue. Excuses were unnecessary. The man was observant enough to tell she'd lost her appetite and to no doubt guess which part of their earlier conversation had caused it. Most of the time she was able to keep her unhappy past at bay, but once in a while, like today, it reared up and bit her hard enough to draw figurative blood all over again.

Watching him scoop up a messy Freddy and hold him at arm's length, Zoe was touched. Her son was giggling instead of fighting the cleanup and Linc was grinning as if he, too, was having fun. Soapy water splashed the counter and Freddy's shirt, but Linc dried everything off before setting the boy on the floor and telling Star it was okay to play.

When he resumed his seat at the table, Zoe took a

bite of her now-cold pizza just to please him. "I'm really not hungry."

"Well, maybe you will be later. Want me to slip the leftovers into your fridge?"

"Sure. That would be fine. Don't bother wrapping them. They never last long enough to get stale."

Linc had put the pizza away and was straightening when she saw him pause and apparently listen to his earpiece. He touched the mic on his shoulder. "Copy. Did you take a report?"

Again, he listened, making Zoe curious. It wasn't until he had ended his one-sided conversation that she asked, "More trouble?"

"Not about your brother, if that's what you mean. Do you know Yvette Crenville? She's the base nutritionist."

"I think I may have met her. Why?" Zoe held her breath, hoping he wasn't going to cite more mayhem. "Is she okay?"

"Yes. But she reported harassment, so I wondered if there might be any connection to your problems."

"Who bothered her?"

"I suppose it won't hurt to tell you since she says it's already shown up on that unauthorized base blog we've been trying to silence."

"The one that claims to have all the inside info on Boyd and blames me for keeping his whereabouts a secret?"

"Yeah, and insists your encounters with prowlers are fake and meant to distract us from tracking him. Whoever's been writing it apparently keeps shutting down in one place and popping up in another before we can get a handle on the location. I suppose if the brass gave it high priority, they could stop it, but so far it's proved fairly unimportant. It is bothersome, though."

"No kidding. What's the story on Yvette?"

"She says she's afraid of one of the aircraft mechanics. Jim Ahern."

Zoe smiled slightly. "That guy may think he's a priceless gift to all women, but he seems pretty harmless."

She had expected Linc to ease up and was taken aback when he frowned instead. "What's wrong?"

"Ahern was one of the only other people who visited your brother in prison. We checked him out thoroughly, but since his name has popped up again, maybe we need to keep a closer eye on him." He sat down at the table opposite her, his eyes never leaving hers. "Remember I told you I found out from one of Boyd's cell mates that he had a burner phone? A lifer named Johnny Motes. He told us that the calls Boyd had made sounded more businesslike than romantic, so we figured he was contacting cohorts on the outside."

"What makes you believe anything a convict says? He could have lied."

"Yes, he could have. But Motes was negotiating for a better pillow and five hundred bucks in his commissary account, so we figured he was probably on the up-and-up. If I hadn't been so sure he was being truthful, I wouldn't have come up with the five hundred myself."

"*You* paid it?"

"It was that or not get the whole story. I thought it was worth taking the chance, and the air force didn't agree."

"So, was my brother contacting Ahern? He's here on base. He could easily have helped Boyd."

"True, but the unproven suspicions regarding Ahern are for petty crimes and vandalism. Besides, as you said, he's a great mechanic. Why would he risk his air force career?"

"Him?" She jumped to her feet. Anger had taken over. "What about *me*? I love the air force. I worked hard to get to where I am, and I intend to stay until retirement. Why would I do something that would cost me so much?"

"Whoa. Calm down." Speaking quietly, Linc joined her and reached for one of her hands.

She jerked it away. "Why should I calm down? The whole base has been treating me like a leper ever since Boyd showed up and started doing his Red Rose Killer act here. You Security guys have made me the main focus of your investigation. All that does is convince everybody that I'm a part of his crimes."

"It isn't just that. Really. Listen to me. My assignment may have started out as a normal surveillance of your activities but it has turned into more, at least for me."

Once again, he reached for her hand, and this time Zoe didn't pull away. "Explain."

"It's beginning to look as though you may be the target of some dirty tricks, okay?"

"You mean like opening my apartment door and leaving it ajar?"

"That and maybe the guy with the knife, not to mention your fake chauffeur this morning."

"Have they located him?"

"No, but one of the cars had additional miles on it so we had it dusted for prints. It had been wiped down."

"Wonderful. Just like my apartment and that warehouse door. Why can't crooks be as dumb in real life as they are on TV?"

"They all make mistakes eventually. The trick is never giving up and following every lead."

Zoe couldn't help being bummed. "I suppose nobody is looking for the redheaded shooting victim I saw."

"Not that I know of. Do you think that was a setup, too?"

"It almost had to be to leave no clues. I've been over and over what happened that day and I still can't figure out why anybody would want to stage a fake murder or would have known I was in that warehouse and in position to see it."

"We came to the same conclusion."

"Unless you weren't the only one following me."

"Star never alerted."

"Yeah." She sighed noisily and gestured around the room. "Like in here, this morning."

"Not exactly. She did seem to hit on trails, but they were pretty much all over the place."

"Could she have been mistaken?"

Zoe felt his fingers tighten around hers and noticed a hardness in his gaze that indicated intensity she couldn't explain until he said, "No. I think she was picking up the scent of somebody who had been walking around inside your apartment and had covered a lot of ground." He paused, then added, "I suspect whoever has been in here may have been doing things to try to convince you you're losing your mind."

"Gaslighting me? Why would they do that? Are you joking?"

The somber way Linc shook his head told her otherwise. "No. The more I think about it, the more sense it makes. I want you to start keeping track of every time you notice an anomaly. I don't care how insignificant it is. Write it down along with the time of day and the date. We need to see if there's a pattern."

Zoe would have pulled her hands free and gone to get a pen and paper right then if she hadn't been so comforted by Linc's touch. A few more seconds of drawing strength from him wouldn't make any difference in the long run. Some of the instances of confusion were etched in her memory while more minor ones had been forgotten. They could start with her stronger memories and build from there.

Raising her gaze to his, she was met by a softening of his green eyes and the promise of a smile. Her lower lip trembled, as did the hands he was grasping.

"It's going to be all right," he told her.

When he put it that way and looked at her with such gentle strength, she didn't doubt him for a second.

His lips were so close, his manner so inviting, she had to struggle to keep from rising on tiptoe and kissing him. Their clasped hands formed a barrier between them that was helping to keep them apart, until he released her and bent to close the distance.

Zoe closed her eyes and gave in just as Linc apparently gained control of himself and pulled away. To her embarrassment, she almost staggered forward to kiss empty air.

He caught her shoulders, righted and steadied her, then smiled sadly as if he'd read her mind. "Not a good idea, I'm afraid."

Moritfied beyond belief, she shook loose and denied everything with a quick reply. "I have no idea what you're talking about."

His laughter as she stomped away grated like spinning tires throwing up loose gravel.

It wouldn't have been so bad if he hadn't been right.

NINE

Star was napping on the sofa beside Freddy, but Linc was so uptight by the time Zoe finished relating all the questionable instances of the past few weeks he had to pace.

Reaching the boundary of the small living room, he spun around to face her and pointed at the tablet on the kitchen table in front of her. "I can't believe you didn't bother to mention all this."

"Most of it could have been my imagination. You said yourself that I've been under a lot of stress."

"Forget that. Think. See yourself as the victim and assume all these things were done to unsettle you. Who would be that vindictive?"

She huffed and arched both eyebrows. "Lately? There isn't enough paper on this pad to list the names of all the people who seem to be upset with me. Ever since Boyd showed up at Canyon Air Force Base and my name was linked with his, I haven't even had an invitation to go out for coffee."

"You're exaggerating."

"I wish I were. I go to work, do my job, come home to Freddy, then do it all over again the next day. My social life is the pits."

"Unbelievable."

"Yeah?" She rolled her eyes. "Believe it, Colson. Sharing this pizza with you is the closest I've come to having company in weeks." He heard her huff before she continued. "But at least that beats being hit on by airmen who think that just because I'm a single woman I must be ready for romance."

"There is the problem of crossing ranks being forbidden. Don't they understand how much trouble you'd be in if you accepted dates with them?"

Zoe chuckled. "Yeah, well, it doesn't seem to bother them to try. I think it's probably a challenge to see if their macho appeal is enough to get me to step over the line. Most of them are pitiful."

"Gotcha." Linc rejoined her, sat with his elbows resting on the table and pulled the list to him. "I suppose there's no way you can recall names, is there?"

"Mostly, no. A lot of the offenders were my students of course, because I have the most one-on-one contact with those. I think a few even thought they could overturn my decisions to wash them out by romancing me. There were times when it was actually hard to keep a straight face."

"Maybe you're selling yourself short," he said quietly, watching her for clues to her innermost feelings. "There are lots of men on base who would count themselves fortunate to get a date with you."

To his chagrin, she laughed. "I don't see them lining up because I'm such a great catch. And that's for the best. I already told you. I have no intention of getting involved. I have my job and Freddy. That's plenty for a satisfying life."

"I've enjoyed being with you today. That's not a bad thing, is it?"

His ego took a jolt when she looked him straight in the eyes and said, "You're here because you're working. Nothing more, nothing less. When the job is over, you won't give me or my son a second thought, and you know it."

Mentioning their "almost" kiss seemed inappropriate in view of her candid opinion. Besides, Linc began to wonder if the physical attraction between them was merely a result of proximity. After all, he was a normal man and Zoe was a beautiful woman. There was bound to be at least a little overt interest. He certainly couldn't deny that he admired her. She was beyond strong willed and intelligent, not to mention she had integrity.

Finally, he could admit he believed her when she insisted she'd had no recent contact with her nefarious brother. And he also believed that someone was trying to convince her she was mentally unbalanced. Given what she'd already weathered in life, he had to assume she was smart enough to discount such blatant maneuvering. Perhaps it was time to tell her so.

Linc reached across the table the way he had when she'd needed comforting during their meal. Once again, Zoe let him touch her hand. "Look," he said, "I know this is a rough time for you. And I don't deny there's tension when I'm working with you. But that doesn't mean I can't enjoy your company, too. The more I learn, the more I trust you."

"Really?"

"Yes, really. We'll still be keeping an eye on you in case Boyd shows up, but I believe you when you say you had nothing to do with his escape or presence here."

Glistening unshed tears made her eyes sparkle. The urge to reach out with his free hand and cup her cheek was so intense Linc almost acted on it. He thought he'd regained his self-control until a solitary tear slid down her cheek.

Before he could stop himself, he'd brushed it away with his thumb. The sight of the vulnerable, innocent woman reached inside his heart and settled in as if making a home there. This kind of pure empathy was beyond his ability to resist. Without meaning to get in this deep, he had carried out his captain's orders to befriend her. Boy, had he.

The biggest problem Linc had now was how he was going to keep his emotions tamped down enough to properly do his job. This was why family members were seldom assigned together. They mattered too much to each other. And right now, right here, Zoe Sullivan meant more to him than was good for either of them.

His relief K-9 officer showed up on time, removing his reason for staying. Linc was not happy that the night watch had fallen to a rookie. Nevertheless, it was not his place to question his superiors' decisions, so he checked in with the airman, then headed for his quarters with Star.

It was going to be a long night.

The sensitivity Linc had shown when they'd been together in her kitchen had stuck with Zoe long after he'd left.

He'd taken copies of her lists with him, promising to check which of her possible suspects may have been off duty when the majority of her home invasions had taken place. Given the number of them, such a search was going to take time. In fact, she began to wonder whether one perpetrator was responsible for everything.

The more she mulled over her life, the more people she noted who were not happy with her.

Such was the lot of a dedicated instructor whose final decisions about a candidate's flying abilities and reasoning in a crisis could make or break his or her career. The percentage of female pilots she had washed out was about the same as male. Although, with fewer women applying for flight school, the actual numbers were smaller. Then there was the gender bias some of the students had against her. Yes, this was the twenty-first century but old habits died hard, even now. Life off the base in rural Texas was proof of that, although since she rarely ventured into nearby towns, she hadn't often run afoul of good old boys and their antiquated attitudes.

Deep sleep came more easily than Zoe had expected. Freddy had been so tired after the stimulating Sunday he'd had that he'd gone to bed without argument and she had soon followed.

Morning light was beginning to filter through the blinds in her bedroom when she finally stirred. Stretched. Swung her legs over the side of the bed, onto the floor and felt…

Bolting upright, she gasped. Lifting her bare feet, she looked down and her eyes widened with shock and fear. The soles of her feet were covered in a warm, sticky red substance.

Blood.

The smell was so cloying. She started to gag, then forced herself to calm down. To take stock of the situation. *Am I hurt? No.* Nothing physical seemed to be wrong with her. But then where had the pool of blood come from? Whose could it be?

"Freddy!" Zoe leaped up and dashed toward her son's room with no thought of the bloody footprints she was leaving in her wake. A scream lodged in her constricted throat, kept there by sheer force of will as she braced herself to face the worst nightmare of her life. She slid to a stop at her son's open door, one hand on the jamb to steady her trembling body and keep her knees from buckling.

A sigh replaced the scream in her throat when she found Freddy lying on top of the covers in his pajamas, soundly asleep and clearly unhurt. As she watched, he made a sound like a sleepy kitten and rolled over to face her. He was fine.

"Thank You, Jesus," she whispered breathlessly.

Zoe knew he'd be terribly frightened if he saw her feet, so she edged away and turned back, retracing her crimson footprints. The blood wasn't from her or Freddy, so where had it come from? Why hadn't she awakened? Moreover, who had managed to invade her privacy once more to carry out such a heinous act?

Fear-based adrenaline had borne her to her son's room. Now, though, she shook so badly she could hardly continue to move. She leaned on the walls, working her way along until she was back in her own room.

The foul puddle remained beside her bed and she could see where she had initially stepped. A strong urge to wipe up the mess almost overcame her before she reached for her cell phone instead. She must not touch anything. She had to summon help. To call... Linc Colson. No one else would do, not even others on the Security Forces.

Hand still extended, she struggled to subdue her tremors enough to properly pull up his number and

prayed that the strong stomach on which she prided herself wouldn't fail her. An unexpected vibration almost
caused her to drop the phone before she could dial. She
was receiving an incoming call. From Linc!

All self-control fled the moment she heard his voice.
Before he could finish his good-morning greeting, she
was shrieking unintelligibly. It was the closest she could
come to shouting, "Help me!"

Linc had been standing in the street observing her
apartment window when he'd called. There was no way
to tell what Zoe was trying to say, but he didn't need
words. Her shrillness and sobbing were plenty.

"I'm coming!" Phone pressed to his ear, he straight-
armed the outer door and raced up the stairway. Star
was way ahead of him. He noted a fleeing figure
dressed in black at the far end of the hallway and made
the split-second decision to drop the leash, point and
command, "Get 'em!"

Training dictated he must follow his K-9. And he
would have. If Zoe had not appeared in her doorway
with both feet covered in blood.

Linc's heart and gut clenched simultaneously. Sliding
to a halt he shouted, "How bad?" as he eyed her from
head to toe, expecting to see injuries. Would his skills
be sufficient to save her life if she was bleeding out?

"It's—it's not mine," she stuttered. Arms extended,
palms up, she simply stood there as if in shock.

"What do you mean it's not yours?" Linc's already-
taut muscles knotted more. He could barely get
"Freddy?" out or believe Zoe when she shook her head.

"No. Not him either."

"You *sure*?"

"Yes. I just checked. I don't know where this awful stuff came from. There's a big puddle of it in my bedroom."

Linc saw her start to waver as if she might faint. He reached out, ready to steady her if need be, yet failing to fully grasp her explanation. She was panting as though she'd just finished a marathon and her eyes weren't focusing well. They were wide and glassy.

He reached for her. She started to pull away and staggered. Linc caught her by the arm. "You need to sit down." Truth to tell, so did he.

"I—I—I woke up and…"

"This happened while you were asleep?"

Another nod.

"Did you see anything, anybody?"

"No. I'm a sound sleeper except for sometimes when Freddy makes a noise at night. I never heard a thing."

"Okay." He guided her all the way inside, preparing to close the door behind them.

She started to fight him. "Let go. I need to wash. I have to get this off me!"

There was panic in her tone. Little wonder. Though Linc commiserated, he stopped her. "No. You can't wash until the crime scene techs get here. We'll need pictures of everything in situ. I mean, where it is now."

In the background, he heard Star barking ferociously. She had someone cornered. "I need to go help my dog. Will you be okay?"

Zoe nodded and leaned against the doorjamb. "Yes. Go. Catch whoever did this and bring him back so I can take a good swing at him."

"Atta girl. I mean, affirmative, Sergeant."

Star's barking reached a crescendo. Linc knew that

as soon as it stopped she'd capture her prey with a painful bite and be holding fast until given the command to release.

His boots hit the floor hard, the sound echoing along the empty hallway, reminding him of a beating heart. His own was pounding, more from seeing what had been done to Zoe than from actual exertion.

Star gave one last intense growl before a human screamed. She had him! *Good girl*, Linc thought. *Hold.*

The screams turned to curses. Almost to the corner where he'd last seen his K-9 partner, Linc heard a scrambling sound followed by Star's yip. Then all was silent.

He whipped around the corner so fast he almost lost his footing.

For the second time in minutes his heart stopped. There lay his dog, alone and prostrate. It took several more seconds before Linc was close enough to tell she was still breathing. Falling to his knees beside her, he gently touched her quivering side.

"I should have stayed with you," he whispered haltingly. "I'm so sorry, Star."

TEN

Mayhem reigned in and around Zoe's apartment. When Linc didn't return quickly, she'd put in a call to Security Forces and reported all she knew, including the sounds of human and dog doing battle. That would certainly explain why Linc and Star had not come back yet.

Further proof was the arrival of other K-9 teams. Among them was Master Sergeant Westley James, handling an all-black German shepherd, another man with *Watson* on his name tag and what looked like a Belgian Malinois, and a stern-looking guy in a dark windbreaker displaying *FBI* in large white letters across the back.

Zoe stayed out of their way while being examined by ambulance personnel. She'd kept her head enough to insist on photos before allowing the first responders to check her from head to toe. While a young female airman kept Freddy occupied and isolated, crime scene investigators had taken samples from Zoe's bedroom and had bagged everything before allowing her to shower in private.

Getting clean had never felt so wonderful. If she hadn't been so worried about Linc and his dog, she would have felt total relief. No one was telling her a thing. After having got used to the way Linc had begun treating her, she was taken aback by the cold shoulder she got from both his team and other investigators.

Emerging in clean, dry PT clothing and with a towel around her wet hair, Zoe recognized Captain Blackwood from the warehouse investigation. When her eyes met his, she was not soothed in the least.

Nevertheless, she approached him and saluted. "Captain."

His blue steel glance was almost enough to give her the shivers. "Sergeant Sullivan. I'm told you can't explain what took place here this morning."

"Only that I woke up and stepped in—" Zoe swallowed hard "—blood. I have no idea when it was put there or who did it. I didn't see a soul." She watched a shepherd dog leaving with its handler. "Did the dogs turn up any clues?"

"Some. Whoever supposedly attacked you is most likely the same person Star apprehended. A scent trail led from here to the spot where the dog was injured."

Zoe's heart skipped a beat. "She's going to be all right, isn't she? Nobody will tell me a thing except that she's alive."

"I don't have the veterinary report yet, but she was conscious when she was transported."

Clasping her hands, Zoe felt tears welling. "Oh, thank God. Literally. I've been praying for her to be okay."

Blackwood didn't seem impressed by her spirituality. "I would think, Sergeant, that you would put your son's welfare first and stop resorting to cheap tricks. Believe me, we will not be distracted that easily."

"What do you mean, *tricks?*"

"You know as well as I do that the red substance was not real blood."

"What? It wasn't?"

"No. It was not."

"Then why did you take so long examining my apartment?"

"Obviously something occurred here. If you didn't set up this fiasco to throw us off your brother's trail, perhaps you would like to stop withholding information about the person or persons who have been harassing you."

"Is that what you call it? I call it attacking me, especially this last time. That stuff sure felt real. How was I to know it was fake?"

He studied her as if she were a slide under a microscope before saying, "We're running tests on it to see if it can be traced, not that that will help much."

Zoe didn't try to suppress a shiver. "There's nothing more I can tell you, Captain. If I'm free to leave, I plan to drop my son at day care early, then begin conducting my regular classes. Any objections?"

"Not from me. When you're not teaching, Master Sergeant James will make sure you're covered until Sergeant Colson is able to resume his regular duties."

"Will that depend on Star? I mean, does she have to be well before he can come back to watch me?"

"That will be up to Sergeant James. As long as Sergeant Colson isn't involved in aggressive tracking or apprehension, I see no reason why he'd be sidelined until his K-9 is fit for duty."

"Thank you." Zoe truly meant it. The captain might not be smiling but at least he was speaking to her. She thought of teenage Portia and felt a twinge of empathy. It was hard for her, being of a lower rank, to speak openly with Blackwood. What must it be like to be his daughter and be forced to get used to his stern demeanor as part of daily life at home? Nightmares were made of notions like that. Although, given her own dad's overly permissive attitude toward his only son when Boyd was a naughty child, she guessed she'd rather have a strict father like the captain.

"Too bad we don't get to choose our parents," she murmured as she headed for her room to dress for work. In a way, she could choose another parent for Freddy, couldn't she? By finding a suitable male role model for her son while he was young and impressionable, she could help him mature into a far better man than her brother ever thought of being.

So who's a good candidate? It didn't take a heartbeat for her to picture Linc Colson. *Except I'm never getting married again*, she insisted. *Never, never, never.* Freddy can have mentors without her marrying them. Besides, limiting his exposure to one man was too exclusive. He needed to meet lots of strong, honest, sensible yet gentle men.

And there it was again. The image of Linc burning brightly in her thoughts and memories.

Logic intruded to dampen her mood like a summer thunderstorm in the dry Texas hills. Colson was only hanging around because he had orders to. Now that he'd been through trials with her, seen her looking her worst and had his dog injured to boot, she'd be the last woman he'd be able to look at romantically, even if she so desired.

Which I do not, Zoe insisted, hoping that stating the obvious would help her accept it. If she ever did decide to remarry, she knew she would choose a man a lot like Linc. *Except with a more trusting nature*, she added quickly. She might have a ton of baggage left over from childhood, but Colson wasn't empty-handed either. They were both toting enough excess to fill the cargo hold of a C-130.

Little feet pattered. Freddy ran to her as soon as she entered his room. He tugged on her skirt. Zoe bent down. "What, honey?"

"I'm hungry."

"I know you are, Freddy. What do you say we go out for breakfast today?"

"Why?"

"Um, because the house is a mess and there are lots of people here."

"I saw. They made me stay in my room." He brightened. "You can make pancakes for them, too!"

"No, thanks." Zoe helped him put on socks and shoes, then lifted him into her arms. "We can stop and buy breakfast on the way to see Miss Maisy at day care, okay? You can order whatever you want."

"Where's Star?"

Zoe had been hoping he wouldn't ask, but she wasn't going to lie to him. "Star got a little boo-boo so she's at the doctor's."

"Will he give her a shot?" The child's fearful expression was so comical she almost laughed.

"I don't know, honey, but if she does get a shot, I'm sure she'll take it like a good airman."

"Yeah. She's real brave."

Braver than I am sometimes, Zoe thought with chagrin. While she'd been standing there feeling sorry for herself and inadvertently distracting Sergeant Colson, that amazing K-9 was chasing down whoever had messed with her. If she were authorized, she'd award Star a medal.

Even though the blood wasn't real.

At the Military Working Dog Training Center, in the veterinary hospital wing that was an integral part of the installation, Linc's injured rottweiler lay stretched out on a steel table in an exam room. She was conscious and panting but not her usual energetic self.

Linc hovered in the background while Captain Kyle Roark, DVM and head of Canine Veterinary Services at CAFB, went over Star, wet black nose to stubby tail. One young female tech dressed in blue scrubs stood by, waiting for orders while another was preparing a gurney.

"I've given your dog a mild sedative and painkiller," Roark said, turning a sympathetic gaze toward Linc. "Her overall condition is good, but her respirations are a little fast and shallow." He was using a light but firm touch to examine Star's body. "I don't feel any broken bones, but I'm going to have Airman Fielding take her down to X-ray to make sure her ribs aren't cracked. Why don't you come with me and get a cup of coffee while we wait for the results of the films?"

"I thought they were digital these days."

Roark chuckled. "They are. It's an old habit to refer to plates and actual film." He stripped off latex gloves and dropped them in a refuse bin before taking Linc by the arm and steering him out of the exam room.

"I should stay with Star," Linc said. "She needs me."

"What she needs is rest, which I will see she gets while she's here. Don't worry. My people know what they're doing. Fielding may look young and afraid of her own shadow sometimes but she knows her job and does it well. You need to back off and settle down before your dog picks up your nervous vibes and gets upset herself."

Although Linc walked the hallway with the doctor, his heart remained with his K-9. "It's all my fault," he said solemnly when they reached the break room. "I stopped to check on a human victim and let Star go on alone. I should have stayed with her until we'd apprehended the suspect."

"Not if you thought you had a victim at the scene already. You know the dogs are trained to bite and hold on. The fact that Star took a couple of hits before he stunned her and escaped proves how good that training is."

"There's nothing wrong with my dog," Linc said, grimacing. "It's *my* training that needs refreshing."

The dark-haired veterinarian chuckled and clapped him on the back. "Don't be so hard on yourself. She's going to recover. The X-rays are just to be on the safe side. If it is cracked ribs, it's nothing life-threatening."

"If I ever catch up to the lowlife who kicked her, there'll be something life-threatening for him. *Me.*"

"Spoken like a dedicated K-9 handler." The vet approached a coffee urn and slipped two Styrofoam cups off the stack, handing one to Linc. "Help yourself. Creamer and sugar are over there."

"Thanks. I didn't get my usual shot of caffeine this morning." He filled his cup. "I was planning to have coffee with Sergeant Sullivan."

"I gather there's a big mess over there?"

"Yeah." Linc was shaking his head as he followed Roark to a small table, plopped into a folding chair and wrapped both hands around his steaming cup. "I thought the sergeant had been cut to pieces when I first saw her." He suppressed a shudder.

"So I understand." The captain's dark gaze narrowed on the sergeant. "What's the deal with you and her, anyway?"

"Sullivan? Nothing special. Master Sergeant James ordered me to stick close and see what I can learn by finessing information out of her."

"Uh-huh." Folding his muscular arms across an equally strong chest, Roark began to grin. "You sticking with that story?"

"It's true."

"Right. And I'm the commander in chief." His expression of good humor softened. "There's nothing wrong with two sergeants becoming involved. At least you're not breaking any rules if you decide to date her."

"It's not like that. I'm just taking most of the daytime watches so she'll get comfortable with me and open up." He made a face into his coffee cup instead of looking at the captain. "I have decided she's not hiding info about her brother."

"So you trust her?"

"Enough. She's got a little boy. I don't think she'd do anything that might put him in jeopardy." A flash of pain crossed the vet's face so briefly that if Linc had not been looking straight at him he would have missed seeing it. "Hey, sorry, Captain. I wasn't thinking."

Roark shrugged nonchalantly, but Linc wasn't fooled. The memory had hurt. "It's okay. It happened a long time ago."

Knowing that the man had lost both his wife and a young daughter—and during the Christmas season to boot—Linc decided to change the subject. "What's the prognosis for Star? Do you think she'll be side-lined long?"

"I doubt it. If nothing's broken, she should get over any soreness in a few days or so. Even with cracked ribs, she can do light duty." His smile returned. "I don't recommend you send her on any more solo chases for a while, though."

"Yeah. My fault entirely."

"What about Sergeant Sullivan? Did she sustain any injuries in the attack?"

Linc shook his head. "That's the crazy part. Whoever broke into her apartment apparently did it to unhinge her. I'm actually surprised that she recovered enough to function this morning."

"Women are not the weaker sex, in case you haven't noticed. We may be physically stronger, but they have us beat when it comes to rolling with the punches. Look at how she refuses to be cowed by a murderous brother. I'd have my back to a wall and be locked and loaded 24/7 if Boyd Sullivan came from my family. My older sister is bad enough." His smile spread to a grin. "She's a major in the army."

"Wow. I see what you mean."

Relaxing in the chair and stretching, Roark asked, "What about your kin, Colson? Are they military, too?"

Linc wished he could find a hole in the floor and dive through it. "One was. We don't talk about him."

"Don't worry about it," Kyle Roark said. "Every family has its unsavory relatives. You just have to dig deep enough and there they are."

"Yeah." Thinking of Zoe, Linc asked, "Do you know anything about Sergeant Sullivan's late husband? His name was Flint. John Flint."

"Not offhand. Why?"

"It's not important. Apparently, he wasn't the finest representative of the air force either."

"We take what we can get," the vet replied. "Some recruits are better than others. Take Airman Fielding, for instance. At first glance, she seems a bit on the flighty side, but she's the best tech I've had in years."

"What's her story?"

Roark shrugged. "Beats me. She's not a typical chatty female. When I'm doing surgery that's a plus, believe me."

Linc stood, disposed of his empty Styrofoam cup and waited for his companion to join him. "I'm ready to go back and see about Star."

"Okay, okay. We've had a long enough break, anyway." He clapped Linc on the shoulder. "Remember what I said about women. It's okay to take up with somebody of equal rank. You won't lose stripes over it."

"That's not what's stopping me."

"Oh?" They proceeded down the short hall together.

"Marriage is not for me. Never was. Never will be."

"Sounds pretty final."

"It is. Just because I believe she's been truthful about her brother doesn't mean I trust her regarding all the harassment she's receiving. She keeps insisting she has no idea who's doing this to her, yet it seems irrational that she wouldn't have at least a glimmer of a clue."

"You've classed her as an honest person, right?"

"Right." Not sure what the captain's point was, Linc waited for more.

"Then maybe she's too forthright to recognize lies coming from those around her. I've known people like that. They have trouble seeing beyond the good and grasping the bad in others."

"Naive, you mean?"

Sobering, the captain led the way into his office and gestured toward a leather chair. "Have a seat."

"What about Star?"

"They'll notify me when she's ready for further examination. I want to talk about you for a minute." He circled his desk, sat down, pushed aside a short stack of files and clasped his hands atop the blotter.

"Okay." Given no other choice if he intended to see his K-9 soon, Linc eased into the chair Roark had indicated.

"Tell me about your combat experiences."

"Whoa. Where did that come from?"

"I'm getting the idea that there's more to your decision to stay single than you've admitted, that's all. Would you like to talk about it?"

A wall immediately rose around Linc's emotions. He knew he could refuse to discuss his past, and seriously considered doing so, yet there was something about Kyle Roark's manner and voice that urged him to open up. If the captain had pressed him, he was positive he could have held out. Since Roark merely waited and seemed relaxed about it, he decided to reveal a little.

"I lost part of my unit in Afghanistan."

A nod. "Understood."

"We were acting on bad intel and walked into an ambush. I barely got out alive. Some of the guys didn't."

"Not your fault, was it?"

"Not directly. We'd been befriended by the most beautiful dark-eyed woman I'd ever seen. Even with her hair covered, she was a stunner." Swallowing hard, he struggled to go on. "I wasn't the only one who fell for her lies. She was easy to believe."

"Again, that's not your fault. I'm sure she was well trained in fooling the enemy."

"Well, she was good at it. We followed her advice and walked right into a trap."

"You can't classify all women as liars because one tricked you. That's a lousy reason to reject romance."

"It's not just her," Linc countered. "It's a lot of things. My dad was the best liar I've ever known. He had everybody convinced he was some kind of hero when he was anything but."

"Sociopathic, maybe?"

"Maybe." Getting to his feet, Linc began to pace. "Look, I appreciate your concern, Doc, really I do, but all I want to do is be the best at my job and handle the best dog. Star and my badge are all I need. Deeper involvement with a subject I'm assigned to watch would be idiotic."

"So, how about somebody else?"

"Not interested."

Chuckling, the veterinarian rose and followed Linc to the office door. All he said was "Uh-huh. That's what I thought."

ELEVEN

Wearing her spotless dress uniform instead of her camo ABU, Zoe squared her shoulders, briefcase in hand, smoothed her blue skirt below the white blouse and strode from the parking lot to her classroom, expecting it to already be at least half-filled with students. Instead, it was empty.

Confusion momentarily halted her in her tracks. Where was everybody? Surely, she hadn't made a mistake about her duty schedule. That was impossible.

A tall, distinguished lieutenant general in uniform, his chest heavy with medals, appeared behind her at the door and cleared his throat. Zoe turned and snapped to attention with a brisk salute. "General Hall."

"As you were, Sergeant Sullivan. I came by to tell you we won't be needing you here today, or until whatever problems you have with your stalker are resolved."

"But, sir—"

"No buts. I sent you a memo after the final decision was made, but I thought it only fair to deliver this news in person, as well. You're officially relieved of duty until further notice."

Zoe was stunned. She hadn't done one thing to deserve being sidelined. Not one thing. Except be an innocent victim. Didn't the brass realize that?

There was nothing to do but submit, like it or not. "Yes, sir. What's my alternate assignment?"

"You have none. Not for the present. You're free to go wherever you wish on base. Just don't leave."

Realizing that she was gaping at the officer, she snapped her jaw closed. Clearly, there was going to be no chance to present an argument. She saluted again despite her disappointment. "Yes, General Hall."

"That's all. You're excused," he said before turning on his heel and leaving.

Zoe stood there, still and mute, while her temper threatened to come to a boil. The brass were blaming her, too, same as the enlisted members did. Everybody and his brother thought she was breaking rules and running amok when all she was trying to do was live a peaceful life and teach to the best of her ability. Only now they weren't going to allow her to do that either, were they?

She internally shook herself, refusing to be a victim of crime or of her superiors' decisions. What steps she would take next were unknown. The only thing she was sure of was that she wasn't going to sit on her hands and stew when she could be taking action. *Any* action. If she had to poke around in the lives of those she suspected might be holding a grudge and reveal who her nemesis was without help or sanction, then so be it. As long as Colson continued to accompany her, she figured she'd be safe enough leaving familiar surroundings.

Zoe didn't know where she'd have to look or who her snooping might upset, nor did she care. She was already persona non grata on base. A few more ruffled feathers wouldn't hurt a bit.

Heels clicking on the hard floor, briefcase swinging

at her side, she waited until she was out in the warm sunshine before making a call on her cell phone.

Linc Colson answered almost immediately.

"This is Sergeant Sullivan," Zoe said. "Sorry to bother you. How is Star? Freddy's worried." She paused, then finished with the full truth, "So am I."

"I'm still at the vet hospital waiting to hear," Linc said. "Captain Roark thinks she may have cracked ribs, but otherwise she's looking pretty good."

"When will you know for sure?"

"Soon. Why? Has there been more trouble?"

"Yes, in a manner of speaking. I've just been relieved of duty. No more teaching or anything else until we figure out who's been making my life miserable."

"You're not teaching any classes today?"

Zoe could tell by his tone that he was worried and she understood why. She wasn't exactly fond of the decision to sideline her either. "Not today or anytime in the foreseeable future according to Lieutenant General Hall. It's the pits."

"Where are you?"

"I just left my empty classroom. Why?"

"Because you need protection, especially if you're going to be wandering around the base. I'll call my headquarters and arrange an escort until I get through here."

"I don't need a guardian to just go home." Hesitating, she said, "Tell you what. Why don't I come to you? That way I'll know how Star is as soon as you do, and we can leave there together when you're ready."

"I don't know. It might be hours."

"Ha! As if I had plans." Shaking her head even though he couldn't see her doing it, she added, "I'd rather hang out with you than have to break in a new bodyguard."

His muted chuckle came through. "*Break in?* Is that how you see our interaction? I'm not sure I like that opinion, Sergeant. It's not very flattering."

"Okay. How about if I admit how scared witless I was this morning and appeal to your sympathetic nature? I desperately need a friend—or at least somebody who doesn't view me as crazy or dangerous. Or both." Zoe lowered her voice and softened the tone. "I can't explain it any better than that, Colson. This hasn't been the worst day of my life—yet—but it's running a close second or third."

"All right. Do you know where the base dog-training complex is located?"

"Yes."

"I'm at the vet hospital between it and the enlisted rec center. You can't miss it. And don't try to walk all this way no matter how much you love Texas weather. Take a cab."

Smiling into the distance, Zoe could barely glimpse flags flying on the far side of the base. If she'd been clad for running or PT, she might have left her car behind and considered a brisk walk. Dressed in her uniform and the matching pumps that the outfit called for, however, she was far less inclined to go for a long hike, even on sidewalks.

"No worries," Zoe told Linc. "I drove over here this morning so I could drop off Freddy at preschool."

The temporary silence on the other end of the line gave her pause. She scowled when Linc said, "Tell you what, either I'll come pick you up or you need to take a cab."

"Why? I told you I have my car."

His sigh was audible. "Yeah. You parked it there, right?"

"Of course, I did. I couldn't very well stuff it in my briefcase and carry it into class with me."

"Meaning it has sat unguarded for how long?"

"Just a few minutes." She looked at her watch. "Maybe fifteen at the most."

"Call a taxi."

The finality of his command jolted her rather than inciting anger. "You think somebody did something to my car? Why here? Why not back at my apartment?"

"One, we kept an eye on it there and two, that parking lot is always real busy. The place you parked this morning is far more isolated." He cleared his throat. "Humor me, Zoe. Be on the safe side. Call a cab. And do it now, before word gets around that you've been relieved of duty and your enemies start to figure out your new behavior patterns."

"I really hate feeling so vulnerable."

"I know. And I'm sorry. I'd be there right now if Star hadn't got hurt."

"I'm the one who should apologize. You're worried sick about her, and here I am causing you even more problems. I'll be there ASAP. Watch for my taxi."

"Thanks," Linc said.

She could tell he meant it. "No, thank you, Sergeant. You may be the only one on base who believes in me. I do appreciate it."

"The cab," he said gruffly.

"Gotcha. Hanging up now and dialing a ride."

Despite the first pangs of an impending headache, Zoe did as she'd promised. Then she slowly approached her parked sedan and gave it a once-over, even leaned sideways to peer under it. Nothing seemed tampered with or added.

Before her life had been so disrupted, she might easily have pulled out her keys and driven despite Linc's dire warning.

Now she wouldn't touch that car if her life depended upon it. She straightened, fighting an unexpected wave of dizziness. And little wonder. If Linc was right, her life actually might depend upon following his orders. She wasn't about to ignore his advice and test the concept.

When Linc completed the call, he noticed Captain Roark's arched eyebrows, so he explained. "Sergeant Sullivan is coming here since I can't go to her right now."

Roark shrugged. "You could, you know. Star is in good hands."

"I suppose so," Linc said, "but my CO told me to stay with her until I could make a detailed report on her condition. We assumed Sullivan would be secure while she was teaching."

"I take it she isn't?"

Shaking his head, Linc said, "She may be safe enough but she isn't teaching. They relieved her. I don't understand why. She hasn't done anything wrong. Everything's circumstantial."

The veterinarian grinned. "Never try to reason out orders from up top, Sergeant. You'll drive yourself crazy if you expect them to always make sense."

"Gotcha." He eyed the doorway, wishing the tech

would hurry up with those X-rays. "What's taking so long?"

"Tell you what. Why don't you go wait out front for Sergeant Sullivan while I see about your dog? If I need you, I'll send for you."

"That makes sense, I guess." There was no way Linc could divide himself in two, so tending to one task while Roark followed up on another seemed the wisest choice.

Taking a deep, settling breath of fresh Texas air once he reached the sidewalk, Linc was struck by the conundrum he'd just acknowledged. A few weeks ago, there would have been no hard choice to make. He would have opted to remain with his K-9 partner and let someone else fill any other gaps.

Now, however, he saw that his loyalties were being divided, and he didn't like it. In his mind, he visualized being at war with himself, as if he were both friend and foe in an ongoing battle in which there could be no clear-cut winner. If he directed all his energy toward Star and neglected taking care of Zoe and her little boy, he chanced letting harm come to them. If, on the other hand, he concentrated on the woman and child too much, he could lose Star, as present circumstances painfully demonstrated.

Almost convinced to turn and go back inside, he spotted an approaching taxi. To his chagrin, his heartbeat increased in speed and he felt beads of perspiration welling on his forehead. If Zoe was in that cab, then he'd know she was okay. What if she wasn't?

Keying his mic, he radioed Captain Blackwood and identified himself. "I'm still at the vet's. They're taking X-rays of Star. Roark thinks she's okay."

"Good. Call me back when you know for sure."

"I will. But there's been another development," Linc said. "Sullivan has been relieved of duty. She's on her way to join me here."

"What? Why weren't we notified?"

"I imagine we will be. I just thought it best not to wait for the information to go through channels. When she told me, I instructed her to come here instead of my going to pick her up."

"Good. When I told you to get close to the sergeant, I certainly didn't mean for you to abandon your K-9 in a crisis."

"Affirmative. One other thing, Captain. Sullivan's leaving her private vehicle in a parking lot near her classroom."

"Why? Wouldn't it start?"

Linc felt his muscles tighten as if readying for hand-to-hand combat. "That's not the problem. I figured, given the incident at her apartment earlier today, she shouldn't try to drive. She was away from the car long enough for it to have been tampered with."

"Now who's paranoid?" Blackwood asked. "What do you expect me to do about it?"

"I was hoping you'd ask Nick Donovan and his bomb-sniffing K-9, Annie, or somebody from ordnance to take a look. Maybe have it towed to a safe holding area?"

"You honestly think there's a chance it's rigged with explosives?"

"There's a chance of anything at this point," Linc said firmly. "Until we uncover the reasons for the strange attacks on her I think it's prudent to take precautions." He paused. "Listen, she's here, so I have to go. If anything changes, I'll let you know."

"All right. And, Colson?"

"Yes, sir?"

"Keep working on her about her brother. There's a fair chance he's the one behind the weirdness."

"I'll keep that in mind."

"Okay. Now, go see to your dog."

"I will."

Linc smiled and held out a hand to Zoe as she climbed out of the taxi. Her fingers were cool yet as soft as he remembered, her eyes sparkling with delight and her lips lifting in the smile that often graced his dreams of late.

She glanced at the mic clipped to the shoulder of his ABU. "Did you just get another call?"

"No. I was reporting in. Security hadn't been informed of your duty change yet, and I wanted to be sure my bosses were up to speed."

"Good old bureaucracy," she said, grinning up at him. "The news will probably reach interested parties at about the time regular base gossip does."

"Or after." Linc held the glass door to the building open for her. "No troubles getting here?"

"Other than having to abandon my wheels, no," Zoe replied. "I realize that old beater isn't much, but it gets me around okay. I'd hate to lose it."

"I'm having it checked for you," he said. "Until it's cleared, I'll drive you wherever you need to go."

"Thanks." She sobered as they proceeded down a long hallway. "How's Star?"

"No report yet, but it shouldn't be long." Ushering her into the office where the head veterinarian sat behind his desk, Linc saluted and said, "Captain Roark, this is Staff Sergeant Zoe Sullivan."

The captain rose and returned the salute as Zoe did the same. "My pleasure. I understand you've had a rough morning."

"Yes, sir. You could say that."

"Well, if you need a break, we can always provide puppy therapy."

"Sir?"

Roark chuckled. "It's a standing joke around the kennels. Five minutes sitting in a pen of happy puppies is our standard cure for the blues. Works every time."

"My son would love it."

"I'm sure he would." The vet sobered and gestured toward a gurney being guided past the open door. "There's Star now. Follow me."

They joined the dog in the closest exam room where Roark displayed the X-rays on a monitor. "Star's X-rays show that nothing is broken, but she was so sore they had to administer a light sedative in order to get her to lie still for clear pictures. She's still pretty groggy."

Linc was surprised when Zoe dropped her briefcase, beat him to the sleepy canine, caressed her head and bent to kiss her muzzle. "Poor baby. I'm so sorry, Star."

Not only did Linc's eyebrows arch, Roark's did, too. The captain spoke first. "I wouldn't try that when Star is fully conscious if I were you, Sergeant Sullivan. She might take your nose off."

"Besides, we don't want her too well socialized," Linc added. "It can take the edge off protective responses."

Zoe backed away, blushing. "I'm sorry. She just looks so pitiful lying there."

Linc huffed to cover his own tender feelings toward the injured dog. "Yeah, well, she won't once the sedative wears off." He looked to Kyle Roark. "How long will she be sidelined?"

"I'd like to keep her here for a day or so, just to be on the safe side. Internal tissue injuries don't show up on X-rays, and since she is indicating pain, I want her monitored."

"Okay. What now?"

"I'll have Airman Fielding take her to Recovery. You can accompany them if you wish, Colson."

"I don't know. I..." His troubled glance lit on Zoe. "Is there anywhere you need to go now that we know Star's going to be all right?" he asked her.

"Yes," she said with a gentle look and slight smile as she stroked the rottweiler's shoulder. "I want us to go with Star, so you can be there to comfort her when she's fully awake."

The surprised glance the veterinarian shot Linc was nothing compared to his own awe. Despite all her problems and the way most of the base had rejected her, Zoe Sullivan's heart remained kind and caring. She'd realized how much he wanted to stay with his K-9 partner and was facilitating it for his sake. And perhaps for Star's well-being, too.

"Lead on," Linc told the vet tech. "We'll follow you."

As Zoe leaned down to retrieve her briefcase, Linc took it from her, then clasped her hand. She didn't try to pull away. Instead, her fingers laced through his. As far as he was concerned, he'd gladly stay connected like that for the rest of the day.

TWELVE

Seeing Star acting so weak made Zoe want to sit with Star on the folded blanket in the kennel run and cradle the poor dog's massive head in her lap. Only her dress uniform stopped her.

Happily, Linc had no such reservations in his ABU and sat beside his groggy dog, legs crossed.

Zoe leaned against the open gate. "Do you want me to close this?"

"Not yet. After she's back on her feet, we'll shut it and leave so she'll rest. Doc says that's what she needs most."

Studying the row of runs she could see from where she stood, Zoe asked, "Is this where all those loose dogs came from?"

"Some of them. We have a lot more room in the Military Working Dog Training Center next door. There are indoor and outdoor housing areas."

"I saw you catch that one dog. How many are still missing?"

Linc continued to stroke and comfort Star. "At last count, twenty-eight. Since almost two hundred were released in the first place, that's a fair capture rate, but nobody understands why four of the best trained K-9s have remained missing. We're all worried about them."

"What I don't understand is why they didn't all just come home. I mean, they're fed and cared for right here. Why run away and stay gone?"

He shrugged. "The theory in some cases is that since they're not well socialized before training and a few are also suffering from PTSD, the wilds of the base beyond our developed areas appealed to them. Remember, dogs are basically pack animals. If they have a strong pack leader, they'll follow him pretty much anywhere."

"But the base is fenced and patrolled."

"True. But we do get an occasional stray coyote inside the perimeter, so it's possible our missing dogs were able to slip out. Or they could be hiding in or around small caves in the rougher terrain the way Westley James thinks they are. There's also thick woods on base. It's been searched, of course, but so far that hasn't helped." Looking up from Star, he caught Zoe's concerned gaze and added, "We'll catch up to them all eventually."

"Will they still be useful after turning feral?"

"I wouldn't worry about overcoming that. Our trainers are the best in the business. They'll be able to handle any setbacks. It'll just take time and patience." He continued rhythmically stroking his dog's shoulder.

"Do you and Star train all the time?" she asked him.

"Practice, you mean? We do our share. Maintaining the K-9's proficiency is one of the requirements for being a handler. We never stop testing our dogs. Everyday patrols and assignments like the one I have watching you are only part of the picture."

He fell silent and concentrated on soothing Star. Zoe listened and heard a rumble. "Is she *snoring*?"

Linc rested his hand lightly on the rottweiler's head and began to grin. "Uh-huh. She's had a rough day."

As he slowly got to his feet and backed away, he laid one finger across his lips. "Let's go and let her sleep."

Whispering, Zoe questioned that decision, "I thought you wanted to stay with her until she woke up."

He eased her out and closed the gate behind them. "That was when she was groggy from the anesthetic. This is pure sleep. See how her breathing has changed? Deepened? And watch her muzzle."

Zoe had to cover her own mouth to keep from giggling aloud. "Her lips flap!"

"I know. I've spent so much time with her I can tell how she feels by observation. She's exhausted but doing okay. And her gums are nice and pink. That's a good sign, too. According to Captain Roark, that means she's not bleeding internally. If she were, it would be evident by now."

Zoe let him cup her elbow and direct her away from the kennels. Their slow passage didn't rouse many of the other patients housed there. They were out of the veterinary hospital before she asked, "Where are we going?"

"First, I'm taking you home and waiting while you change, since you're not on duty anymore. Then I thought we'd go see one of the women your brother threatened."

"I hope she's here on base, because General Hall ordered me not to leave."

"She is," Linc replied. "First Lieutenant Vanessa Gomez is a nurse at the base hospital, and I want to pick her brain about something."

"Really? What?"

He didn't answer until they were in his SUV and had pulled into traffic. "We got a preliminary report on the substance that was found at your apartment this morning."

"They already told me it was fake blood. It was, wasn't it?"

"Yes. Mostly water and corn syrup with red food coloring and a little chocolate syrup to mute the bright crimson."

"Sure had me fooled when I stepped in it. I even imagined it smelled like the real thing."

"Me, too, at first glance. Very realistic. It made me wonder why the person who left it settled for a substitute. I'd think if he wanted to really freak you out, he'd have used the genuine article."

"Maybe it was hard to come by."

"That's one of the details I want to double-check. If Boyd wasn't behind it and the guy who is didn't want to harm anyone, he might have tried to steal blood from the hospital. I actually hope he did because that could give us some clues."

Zoe's eyes widened. "Of course! Why didn't I think of that?"

"Because you teach flying and I'm the cop. Our forensics team figured out what they were dealing with the minute they walked in. Your apartment smelled more like pancakes to them than it should have."

She smirked at him. "So, cop, what can a nurse tell us that we don't already know?"

"Since she was threatened by the Red Rose Killer, I thought she'd have some personal insights, maybe something more than the hospital administration gave us. It is in her best interest to speak freely, especially if she knows of a gap in their blood distribution system."

"Why take me along? I mean, unless you still think

I'm hiding something and want to make me feel guilty, there's no real reason for me to meet this nurse."

"No, there isn't. But you do have to stay with me, and I have a few loose ends I can hopefully tie up without the use of my dog, so you're coming along. I can't just sit around and wait. It's driving me crazy to be idle."

"I understand," Zoe said, averting her eyes to stare out the window as they turned and crossed Canyon Drive. "I don't want you wasting time with me when there are bigger fish to fry. It's just embarrassing to talk to people my brother has hurt or threatened. I hate that I'm related to a serial killer."

"That's definitely not the reason I want you to go," Linc said. "Two heads are always better than one when it comes to spotting anomalies and picking out which ones may be of interest. And you need something to think about besides your own troubles. I figured a diversion might give your brain something to do while your subconscious works on the rest of our unanswered questions."

Zoe had to chuckle. "Sergeant, if my brain got any busier, my head might explode."

"Which reminds me," he said lightly, keeping the conversation from becoming somber, "after giving it a quick look, the bomb boys didn't find anything wrong with your car, but they did tow it in for further examination."

"I hope I can pick it up soon." Linc's SUV was coming to a stop at the curb in front of her apartment and she reached for the door handle.

"Whoa. Not so fast. I'm going to check your apartment before you go inside."

"Why? Your evidence people were still here when

I left for work and probably stayed most of the time I was gone."

"Most of the time isn't good enough. I'll go in first, do a walk-through, then give you the all clear."

She shuddered, thinking of the way her home had looked the last time she'd seen it. "I hope they took away everything that was soiled. I mean, I'd hate to go back up there and find the same awful red mess I left behind—even if it is fake."

"Tell you what," Linc said. "If there are places that need TLC, I'll take care of those while you change. We can leave the hall door open so we don't start any rumors."

She was touched. And wryly amused. "After everything that's happened to me lately, I imagine my reputation is already trashed. Thanks for trying to protect me from gossip, but I'm less afraid of that than I am of finding another attacker lying in wait. You are more than welcome to inspect the apartment and wait there with me, whether my front door is open or closed."

"Thank you," Linc said.

"I'm serious. I trust you implicitly." Zoe realized she meant that from the bottom of her heart. There might be nobody else she could truly count on except Linc Colson. But that was enough. He was enough.

Watching him don his official blue beret as he circled the vehicle to open her door, she had to fight to keep from once again enumerating his many virtues. This was a good, good man. An admirable member of the Security Forces that kept the base safe. Not only could he be relied upon in a crisis, his presence gave comfort when all was in chaos.

Zoe clasped the hand he offered and carefully

climbed down from the truck. His touch was warm, steady, welcome. It seemed as natural as breathing to slip her fingers between his. It was a pity that this kind of supportive contact would cease once Linc's assignment was over.

Given that nebulous peek into the future, she decided to make the most of these brief moments of closeness. He never needed to know how special he was becoming to her, nor did she intend for their camaraderie to blossom into something more, something deeper. She'd been married once. That was enough. God had rescued her in the nick of time or she might have ended up blamed for John's illegal transfer of classified data simply because she was his wife.

Thoughts of marriage melded with images of the strong man walking beside her and she nearly panicked. She gently slipped her hand from his.

It wasn't a lack of interest that caused her to withdraw. On the contrary. She'd broken their physical bond because she did care for him. Far, far too much.

The steps leading to the second-story apartment looked clean to Linc. What they'd find when Zoe opened her door was what worried him. Even if the evidence techs had gathered up all the throw rugs, there were likely to be signs left behind. How involved the cleanup would be depended on how much Zoe had tracked through the rooms while she'd waited for the authorities.

His jaw clenched as he turned the knob. The door was locked. "Do you have your key?"

"Yes." She produced it from a small handbag tucked

inside her briefcase. "Do I have to wait out here, or can I follow you in like before and see what's what?"

"You can come. Just hang back and let me clear all the rooms before you get too curious."

"Yes, Sergeant."

"You may as well call me Linc," he said, stepping over a tacky partial footprint on the hardwood floor. "Where do you keep your cleaning supplies?"

"You—you don't have to mop this up." She was speaking to his broad back as he walked away.

"Do you want Freddy to come home to it?" Linc called from the direction of the bedrooms.

"Of *course* not."

Linc returned and said, "Then stop arguing and get me some rags, at least. Your room is actually the cleanest of all. I guess they took everything from in there as evidence. It's the hallway and this floor out here that caught the worst of the footprints."

"Do we need bleach, too?" Zoe asked.

"That would probably help lighten the red food coloring if it left stains, but the syrup should wipe up easily. I'm truly sorry this happened to you, Zoe."

"Yeah. Me, too."

Linc's gut twisted as he recalled his first impression of her when he'd seen her in her doorway that morning. The sight had stolen his breath and left him temporarily stunned. That was another reason why he hadn't immediately pursued Star. Concern that Zoe was injured had kept him with her. Wrong or right, it had happened, and Linc wondered if his commanding officers suspected the fault in judgment.

Someday he would have to admit what had been behind his mistake. Hopefully, nobody would ask him to explain further. If they did, he was going to have to admit that his personal feelings had got in the way of doing his job at a most critical moment.

That was bad. Really bad. If it happened again and was reported, he could lose a stripe. Or, worse, he could lose his coveted position as a handler.

Linc sighed. Star—his Star—would be given to someone else.

Zoe took the time to spruce up the bathroom where she had showered earlier, careful to leave no trace of red. By the time she donned jeans and a T-shirt and returned to the living room, there was nothing left to mar that scene, either. She smiled at Linc. "Good job. Thanks."

"You're welcome. Ready to roll?"

"I guess so. I'll take my cell in case Maisy Lockwood calls from her preschool and day care. She's a wonderful teacher, but Freddy sometimes begs to come home early and I have to reason with him on the phone."

"You'd think he'd be adjusted by now. How long has he been going to that place?"

"Most of his life. It's not that. It's the rumors flying around. Even the littlest kids pick things up from parents or other caregivers. With Boyd, the talk of the base, I think Freddy's overheard plenty and he's afraid for me."

"He's not the only one," Linc said. "We'll go over your list of possible suspects again when we break for lunch."

"Okay. Can I ask you a question?"

"Sure."

"Are you going to get in trouble for taking me with you?"

"I don't see a problem." Linc eyed her up and down, bringing a new warmth to Zoe's cheeks. "Dressed like that and with your hair down, nobody who doesn't already know you is going to suspect you're Boyd Sullivan's sister."

She smoothed the powder blue shirt over her jeans and turned in a circle. "You think? I figured since I wasn't on duty, this would do."

"Nicely."

Zoe caught the hint of a blush on his face, too. They were acting more like lovesick teenagers than responsible adults, weren't they? "I can change if you want. Maybe put on an ABU?"

"Nope. No camo. You're fine like you are." He led the way to the exit, and Zoe could have sworn she heard him mutter, "Very fine," before he opened the door and stepped out into the hall.

After that, there was no way she could suppress a grin and the incongruity struck her as ironic. Here she was, the sister of an escaped serial killer, the object of some madman who was bent on trying to drive her crazy, relieved of duty and under the thumb of Security Forces, who had blamed her for crimes that had no connection to her normally placid life. So why was she feeling almost elated?

Because Linc had promised to keep her by his side. There was no other plausible answer. He could have requested a replacement, yet he had not. Therefore, he wanted her there, wanted to be with her.

Looking heavenward, Zoe silently asked God what was going on. She didn't have to wait for an answer.

It already lay in her heart. Like it or not, she was falling for Linc Colson. Hard and fast. And there wasn't a thing she could do about it.

THIRTEEN

Linc had no trouble locating First Lieutenant Vanessa Gomez in the critical-care unit of the base hospital. The insignia on his beret and his telltale sidearm and other official gear allowed them to pass through locked doors without delay.

A nod and salute were his reintroduction when he spotted Vanessa. Seeing the petite dark-haired nurse in her element gave him a more favorable opinion of her inner strength.

Vanessa stripped off latex gloves, disposed of them and quickly joined him. "Good to see you again, Sergeant Colson. I hope you've come to tell me the danger is over."

"Sorry, no," Linc replied. He inclined his head to Zoe. "This is Staff Sergeant Sullivan. Zoe, Lieutenant Vanessa Gomez."

The nurse froze. "Sullivan? You're the sister I've been hearing about?"

"Unfortunately," Zoe said with a huff. She offered her hand and Linc was relieved to see the nurse accept and shake it.

"Sorry." Vanessa was frowning when she looked back at Linc. "Okay. If it's not good news, then give me the bad."

"Actually, in regard to Boyd, there's really nothing new. I came to ask more about blood."

"Blood?" The scowl deepened.

"Yes." Zoe explained, "Somebody sneaked into my apartment this morning and poured fake blood on my floor."

"Fake? That's not a surprise. Getting your hands on the real thing can be harder than robbing Fort Knox."

Linc asked her to go over the details for them.

"Sure. It's a real pain. First, we have to log every drop that comes in and goes out, and there's computer cross-checking. Even after the doctor orders a transfusion and a patient signs a consent form, it takes two of us to access supplies. Before blood is administered, everything is rescanned with the patient's records to prevent errors and verified electronically."

"That basically agrees with the info we got from hospital administration, only you provided more details. Thanks." Linc scanned the quiet unit. The air smelled like antiseptic. Privacy curtains were pulled between each bed and patients were eerily quiet while machinery hummed and beeped. The scenario reminded him of the hospital where he and his injured comrades had been taken after the ambush. Lives were on the line here, too. It wasn't fair. Dedicated men who gave their all for a just cause should never be buried under beeping, flashing machines, tubes, wires and white sheets.

He felt a light brush as Zoe slipped her fingers between his and clasped his hand. Hers was tiny compared to his and her grasp was gentle, yet it wasn't just her skin he felt—it was her emotional support. Had his morose thoughts been that evident? Apparently. And as opposed to shunning him as so many other women had when he'd acted depressed, she had reached out. Lifted him with a mere touch. The simple gesture hit him so hard he wanted to weep.

Instead he gave her hand a squeeze and squared his shoulders, reminding himself that he was on duty and the nurse was a target of the Red Rose Killer. This was not the time to let his mind wander or allow painful memories to take over his thought processes. He had a job to do.

There had been a time, years ago, when Linc would have followed that internal affirmation with a short appeal to a higher power for the ability to triumph. He'd stopped doing that when so many prayers had gone unanswered. Like the time he'd prayed for the welfare of his buddies before and after the ambush.

I should have suspected, he insisted for the thousandth time. *Should have had some inkling that it was a trap.*

Ideas swirled in the back of his mind like a tornado of dust rising from the desert. Had he wondered? Doubted? It was not his practice to accept intel without checking its validity. But they'd been ordered to complete their mission ASAP, and there hadn't been time for many precautions.

And since then? Linc asked himself. Since returning stateside and becoming a member of the Security Forces, he'd occasionally wished he had someone close who understood him, who could empathize without pity.

A shiver shot up his spine. His fingers tightened on Zoe's and he realized she was returning the pressure. They should not even be touching let alone holding hands, so what was wrong with him? Nothing that letting go of her wouldn't cure. The moment he loosened his grip, so did she.

While Linc was lost in thought, Zoe gave Vanessa a smile and filled the silence. "I'm truly sorry you're involved, Lieutenant Gomez."

"So am I. I hope they catch Boyd before anything bad happens to anyone else."

Zoe nodded. "We all do. He's the last person I want to see, but I promise, if he gets in touch with me, I'll turn him over to the authorities in a heartbeat."

Vanessa reached for Zoe and patted her forearm. "I understand what you're going through. I have a brother who needs help, too. It's tough."

Linc could tell that the nurse's compassion had deeply affected his companion, because she sniffled and fell silent. He saluted. "Thank you, Lieutenant. Stay safe, okay?"

"I'll do my best. You, too, Sergeants. Both of you."

Rather than draw out their leave-taking and put more pressure on Zoe, Linc turned, placed his hand at the small of her back and ushered her through the double doors and into the hallway.

"You okay?" he asked her.

All she did was nod.

"Come on. Let's grab some lunch at the Winged Java and relax while we go over your list."

"I think we should get it to go and stop back at the vet hospital to spend time with Star," Zoe said as she swiped at her tearstained cheeks.

"Really? You want to do that? Thanks."

Another nod. "Yes. And after I'm done eating, I may want a session of puppy therapy—unless the captain was joking."

"I think I can arrange something," Linc replied. His poignant words of thanks were for more than just her offer to spend time with Star. It was also for her moral support and understanding, for Zoe merely being herself.

In retrospect, Linc wondered if perhaps he didn't also owe his heavenly Father thanks for arranging their meeting and forcing him to get to know her. The more that wild notion bounced around in his brain, the more he began to accept it as probable. It was certainly plausible.

Zoe carried a cardboard holder with their drinks while Linc handled their food and the door when they arrived at the training complex. This time they entered the facility from the rear and slipped through the connecting doors into the animal hospital.

When she saw Star notice Linc, rise and begin wagging her stub of a tail, Zoe grinned. "Whoa. She's up. And she looks much better."

"Sure does." He set the bag of burgers and fries atop a storage bin and opened the door to his K-9's kennel, bending to greet her with a tousle of her ears and a pat on the head. "How you doing, girl? Feeling good again?"

Wiggling from head to toe, the rottweiler circled Linc once, then returned to face him. Rapid panting made her look as if she was grinning as widely as the tech sergeant was. Star did everything except speak English to reassure him.

"I'd say she's telling you she's fine," Zoe said, with laughter underlying the comment. "Where shall we go to eat? I have a feeling that sitting on the floor with her might make lunch a bit trying."

"She's not supposed to touch any food that's not presented properly and accompanied by the right commands, but in view of the unusual circumstances today, you may be right." He straightened and Star took her place at his left, sitting and waiting for orders. "Let's go inside to the break room and eat there. Captain Roark won't mind."

"Are you sure?"

"Positive. He might not look it, but he's a pushover for a needy animal."

"And hungry sergeants?"

Linc laughed as he grabbed the sack of burgers and fries. "Those, too. Come on."

Following closely and bearing their drinks, Zoe couldn't help smiling with satisfaction and gratitude. This was the first time in almost a month that she remembered feeling both happy and safe. It was difficult to even recall how comfortingly dull her former air force life had been since she'd been on her own. Even when Freddy had been born a few months after John's untimely death, she hadn't worried. Her son was the good part of her late husband, the one thing he had given her that she wouldn't have traded for the world. God had taken those unexpected events and brought great joy and perfect companionship out of her loss and sorrow.

And we know that all things work together for good to them that love God, to them who are called according to His purpose, she silently quoted from memory. Despite every obstacle that had risen against her, she had come through to the other side intact. More than intact if she counted Freddy, and she certainly did. Her son was the light of her life.

And, she realized, the stalwart man marching into the veterinary hospital ahead of her was running a close second. Being with Linc, particularly when she was off duty and out of uniform, felt so good, so perfect, she was astounded.

And grateful. Very, very grateful.

Star rested beneath the small out-of-the-way table Linc had chosen for their meal. Her muzzle lay atop his boots as if to make sure he would not move without her knowledge.

Napkin in hand, Linc started to reach toward Zoe's cheek, then pulled back. Unfortunately, she looked up just in time to notice. "Something wrong?"

He knew he was blushing. That or the temperature in the room had suddenly risen dramatically. "Mustard. You've got a little dab right…"

She quickly wiped her face. "Did I get it?"

"Yes." Averting his gaze, he focused on the pad of writing paper on the table between them. "How about students you washed out? Have you listed all those, too?"

"I think so. At least the ones who stayed in the air force. I'm more likely to remember them than the ones like Boyd who failed altogether and were discharged."

"Okay." Linc started to read the names. "I think we can eliminate most of the women, because the sightings we've had were men. Just out of curiosity though, what's your connection to Lieutenant Heidi Jenks?"

"She interviewed me once for the newspaper. I thought she embellished important details, so I complained. She was not pleased to be criticized by a mere sergeant when she's a first lieutenant."

He read names from the list of former flight school trainees whom she'd had to fail. "What about Jones and Carpenter?"

"Gone, I believe. You can check, but I think both are stationed overseas."

"Okay." His index finger moved down the column of names. "Michael Orleck?"

"Last I heard, he'd become an aircraft mechanic, and a good one, too. That was his niche."

"Is he still at Canyon?"

"Far as I know. I think he works with Ahern."

"The same Jim Ahern who visited your brother in prison?"

Linc watched Zoe's hazel eyes narrow. "Hmm. Interesting."

"I thought so. What do you say we put Star back to bed and drive over to the airfield?"

"Suits me. You know I love watching flying, from the ground or air. It makes me feel amazingly free."

"Then you should try parachuting," Linc teased. "It's a real rush." Waiting for her reaction, he was not disappointed when he saw her eyebrows arch dramatically.

"Tried it because I had to. Wasn't thrilled, thank you."

"Why not? You like freedom."

"I also like survival. As far as I'm concerned, there are very few reasons to leave a perfectly good aircraft to go hurtling through space like a duck with a broken wing."

"You should be the writer, not Heidi," Linc said, laughing. "You have quite a way with words."

Zoe, too, chuckled. "I suspect that may have more to do with not having to put on such a perfect front when I'm off duty. It's nice to let my hair down once in a while."

"I noticed. It's pretty when it's loose like that."

"I meant figuratively." She pulled an elastic band from her jeans pocket and gathered her long light brown tresses behind her head before securing them there. "The warm Texas weather makes it hard to leave it down. Nice when winter comes, though. It helps keep my neck and ears warm."

Linc ran a hand over his shaved nape. "I wouldn't know."

"You never had long hair? Not even in your teenage rebel years?"

He shook his head as he gathered up their paper trash while Zoe grabbed the empty drink cups. "I had no time to be a rebel. With my dad AWOL, I felt like the man of the house and tried to act it. As soon as Mom would sign for me, I joined the air force."

"It was a good choice," Zoe told him. "I'm proud you made it work. A lot of fatherless boys don't." She was following Linc and Star out the door leading to the kennels when she added, "I hope and pray my son turns out half as well as you have."

Linc was speechless. Was she serious? She'd sure sounded that way. *Wow.* He bit back an inappropriate quip he might otherwise have used to keep from accepting such high praise. It was one thing to do his job well and serve his country—that was the norm—but to be held up as the perfect adult male example for the little boy Zoe loved with all her heart was something else. Something far beyond regular service.

He busied himself settling Star in her kennel rather than respond to Zoe's statement. No matter what he said in response, it was bound to sound like either bragging or begging for further praise.

Truth to tell, she had just given him the best compliment of his entire life and he didn't know what to do or say, other than to let it pass without comment. He wanted to thank her somehow, to admit how deeply touched he was, yet he refused to reveal that much raw emotion for fear of disgracing himself.

Whether Zoe knew it or not, she had just put a crack in the thick stony wall he'd trusted to keep his heart and his warrior spirit intact.

Now he'd have to make sure he didn't permit her to widen that gap enough to step through or he might never recover.

FOURTEEN

Wind was gusting off the surrounding hills, lifting fine dust and sand that stung Zoe's cheeks as they crossed the tarmac toward an open hangar. North of the airfield, rows of fighters stood in neat lines, forming their own ready ranks.

Linc touched her arm to get her attention and pointed to a sleek aircraft doing touch-and-go landings. "Your student?"

"Maybe. After basic, they're assigned to one of four advanced-training tracks—bomber and fighter, airlift and tanker, advanced turboprop or helicopters."

"That makes sense, I guess."

"It does, particularly when a pilot ends up assigned to fly large transport and tanker aircraft instead of fighter jets."

"Who decides?"

Zoe turned her back to the gusts and used a hand to control wisps of her flyaway hair. "Thankfully, not me."

"Got it." Linc had to hold on to his blue beret to keep it from blowing away. "Let's get inside before we end up taking to the air, too."

A dash for the closest hangar with open doors brought them relief. No mechanics were working on the various aircraft housed there, which was a good thing because an exposed engine full of grit due to the open bay was far from acceptable.

She pointed to an office. "Daily rosters are posted over there. I'll go check."

"Where you go, I go." Linc fell in beside her.

It only took her a few seconds to spot familiar names. "We must be living right. Ahern and Orleck are both on duty in hangar seven."

"Okay. Before we go talk to them, let's set some ground rules."

"A pilot term. Nice."

Linc was chuckling and shaking his head. "Total accident, I assure you. Tell me more about your dealings with Ahern first."

"He's a disgusting braggart. If he was one tenth as wonderful as he thinks he is, he'd have made chief master sergeant by now. That said, he's a wiz with engines. Not as good on advanced avionics but not bad, either. I think younger guys like Orleck handle most of the electronic testing for him."

"Speaking of Orleck, what's the deal with him?"

"He pitched a fit when I washed him out. Once he'd blown off steam, however, he seemed to settle right down. I heard later that he was grateful for the change of direction. That's the beauty of it. We have a variety of great jobs in the air force and if a person tries, he or she can be very happy, successful and satisfied."

"What about you? Are you happy?" Linc asked.

She huffed. "I was, until they unfairly sidelined me. Now not so much."

"What about in the rest of your life?"

Her eyebrows went up as her suspicion increased. "Are you asking about my brother again? Because if you are, remember what I told that nurse. I am not like Boyd. Never was, never will be. I'm not sure why he turned out so twisted, but whatever happened to him, I escaped that negative influence. Maybe it was because we had different mothers."

"I wasn't asking officially," Linc said. "That was more of an existential question. I know you have Freddy and you love him to pieces, but what about the rest of the time? Are you generally happy?"

Deciding how to answer delayed her response. Finally, she paraphrased Scripture. "'I have learned that whatever state I am in, for whatever reasons, to be content.' The apostle Paul wrote that in his letter to the Philippians. He said it much better than I just did, but you get the gist."

"You don't wish things had been different, could be different?"

Zoe wasn't sure what he was actually asking, but she didn't intend to fall into the trap of assuming his query was personal. They had been discussing air force careers, so she replied in that vein. "There were times I thought I wanted to be a combat pilot. Now that I'm a mother, I've decided it's too dangerous. My son only has me."

"No grandparents?"

She shook her head and made a derisive sound. "My late father ruined Boyd by setting a terrible example and being totally convinced his only son could do no wrong. My mother is still living near the old Wadsworth family place in Dill, but she never had the backbone to stand up to Dad. She's even worse in regard to my brother. Maybe she overcompensates because she's his stepmother. All I know is, I would never give her another child to raise. Uh-uh. No way."

"I get it. I love my mom dearly, and she did manage to get me through my teens, but it was more by accident than from making good choices."

Smiling at him, Zoe spoke her mind. "I don't like giving random credit. You can say I'm deluded if you want. You won't be the first. But I firmly believe that God knew us when we were first being formed and becoming babies, just like the Bible says. He saw where we were going and what we'd become from the beginning."

"Then why didn't he stop your brother before so many people died?"

"I don't know." She refused to let him rile her. "I'm clueless about far more than I dream of ever understanding. But that doesn't change my opinion. I can look back and see times where God intervened and saved me. I imagine you could, too, if you'd do it with an unbiased attitude."

"For instance?"

"How should I know what's gone on in your life? As for mine, I'll tell you this. Boyd was already scary when we were kids. I loved him dearly, but I still wonder how many times he thought of murdering me in my sleep.

"And then there was my husband. John was a handsome smooth talker who had me thoroughly convinced he was some kind of super patriot—when he was exactly the opposite. If he had not died when he did, there's no telling how deep into the pit he'd have dragged me and if I'd have been able to climb out, let alone make the air force my career."

"Do you believe his death was accidental?"

Zoe sobered and her eyes flamed with repressed emotion. "That was the official finding."

"And...?"

"It's my belief that his traitorous cohorts got him out of the way when he made the mistake of bragging to me that he was getting away with breaking the law. How they found out doesn't matter. What does is that I went to my commanding officers and reported it. John was dead within a week."

"Then you can't be sure."

With a telling sigh and shrug of her shoulders, Zoe said, "I'm as sure as the encrypted files on his personal computer can make me. If I had not preempted that discovery with my initial report and John had not been removed from my life, I could have been charged with treason or even have met the same fate he did. Then Freddy would have died, too, because I was carrying him at the time."

"So, you really think God rescued you?"

"It makes more sense than random choice, just like knowing the alphabet and being able to spell makes more sense than closing your eyes and banging on a keyboard until a bestseller emerges."

Linc stared at her for the longest time before he said, "Know what scares me?"

"What?"

A lopsided smile began to lift one corner of his mouth. "You're actually starting to make sense."

Her smile mirrored his, then surpassed it. "Of course I am. That's because I'm right."

Along with a half dozen other mechanics, Jim Ahern was working in hangar seven, as scheduled, when Linc led the way with Zoe behind him.

Linc kept it casual as he approached them. "Jim Ahern?"

The senior mechanic laid aside a socket wrench as he turned to face the Security Forces man. "Yeah."

Smiling cordially, Linc offered to shake hands. Ahern swiped his palms against his oily coveralls before accepting.

"Which one is Orleck?"

Ahern snorted. "Why? What'd he do?"

"Nothing that we know of. I just figured it would save time to speak with both of you at once. Were you both here working all morning?"

"Yup." He cupped a hand around his mouth and called, "Hey, Mike. C'mere a sec."

The younger man who emerged from behind the plane was scowling until he saw Zoe standing behind Linc. Then he began to grin. "Hey, Sarge. What brings you here? Are we late getting a trainer ready or something?"

Rather than let her answer, Linc spoke. "Actually, this visit has to do with Sergeant Sullivan."

"Really?" Orleck was grinning at her as if meeting an old friend and Linc wasn't sure he liked such familiarity, although it did indicate no latent animosity.

Ahern was less amiable. "I already told you guys, over and over, I ain't seen Boyd since he begged me to come visit him in prison. It wasn't my idea in the first place, but we'd been buddies before, so I gave in and went."

Linc chose to refrain from mentioning that Ahern and Boyd Sullivan appeared to be more cohorts than everyday friends. If Sullivan hadn't been drummed out of the service early, there was a good chance Ahern would have been sucked further in and have taken the fall for some of their hijinks. The problem was, and always had been, a lack of concrete proof.

"You haven't been contacted by Boyd?" Linc asked him.

"Nope. I know rumor has him here on the base but if he is, I sure ain't running into him." He pointedly stared at Zoe. "What about her? She's his kin." His brow furrowed deeper and his eyes narrowed. "Is she blaming me? Is that it?"

"No. Not at all." Linc struck a casual pose. "What about you, Orleck? Would you know Boyd Sullivan if you saw him?"

"I might. I did see his picture in the base newspaper and on TV. Why? Did he go and kill somebody else?"

"Not lately. Not that I know of," Linc replied. He purposely changed the subject. "So, how do you like being a mechanic?"

"I like it fine." His gaze kept slipping over to Zoe, and his grin was so friendly Linc was disappointed. If he hadn't known better, he'd have suspected the washed-out pilot had a thing for his former instructor.

"You aren't sorry you didn't get to fly?"

Orleck shrugged. "Sure, from time to time. But I get to go along on plenty of test flights and that gives me my thrills. Keeping these birds in the air is what I do best." Once again, his pleasant expression rested on Zoe. "I actually owe it all to you, Sarge. You helped me find a good fit. Thanks."

"You're welcome," she said.

"Well, then…" Linc hitched up his utility belt and holster out of habit and gave each man a nod. "We'll be going. You know who to call if you catch sight of Sullivan."

Ahern chuckled. "Believe me, if I find any red roses lying around, you're the first guys I'm gonna call."

As Linc turned to go, he placed his hand lightly on Zoe's back for moral support and guidance. Yes, she was perfectly capable of walking beside him without interference. And yes, he could have stopped himself. But there had been something in the manner of both men, not to mention those watching from afar, that made him want to publicly declare that she was with him. Not just there, but *with* him.

They were almost outside before she spoke. "I can't imagine Orleck being behind the attacks on me. Can you? He seems perfectly happy here."

Linc agreed. "What about Ahern?"

"Why would he want to harass me? Because he was a friend of my brother's?"

"It makes a little sense."

Brushing back flyaway strands of her long hair, Zoe faced him. "I don't see it. I think we were grasping at straws coming here in the first place."

"You're probably right."

"So, what's next?"

"You hungry?"

She laughed lightly. "Why are you always trying to feed me?"

"It's a Southern custom. We like to eat."

"I thought I detected a Texas twang, but I figured it was because you'd been stationed here long enough to pick it up."

"Nope. Born and raised. Remember the Alamo and all that."

"I get it. Okay, country boy, you can feed me. And this time let's eat at a table with chairs and napkins and plenty of sweet tea."

"Sounds like you've acclimated well, too."

When Zoe looked into his eyes, Linc saw more than he wanted to see. Although she managed a wan smile, there was a telltale glistening of unshed tears pooling in her hazel eyes. "Until my brother escaped and came here, I'd planned to make Texas my permanent home, even after I retired. Now who knows?"

Something inside him urged Linc to open his arms to her and she stepped into his embrace as if it were the most natural thing in the world. It never occurred to him to try to hide their closeness, nor was he embarrassed by it. She needed comforting that he needed to provide. It was that simple. And that complicated.

Closing his eyes, Linc rested his chin on the top of her head and felt her flyaway hair tickling his nose. Thoughts raced through his mind. How could he fix this for her? How could he make it right and continue to protect her? Suppose he was reassigned? Then what?

With great effort, Linc managed to set her away. Grasping her shoulders, he spoke quietly, privately. "I'm sorry. I shouldn't have done that. It's inappropriate."

Zoe sniffled. "Maybe. But it sure felt good."

That was the crux of the problem. "What I mean is, if word gets back to headquarters that you and I are getting too friendly, there's a good chance I may be relieved of this duty."

Remembering what his master sergeant had suggested gave him some solace, but Linc doubted Sergeant James had meant for him to go this far. Nor had he intended to. Genuine fondness for Zoe had grown so easily it had blindsided him.

She took a step away. Then another. "I don't want to lose you," she whispered. "Just tell me how to act and I'll be glad to comply." A tiny smile quirked at one corner of her mouth. "Under most circumstances."

Linc stood tall, almost at attention. "As soon as Star is released for duty, I think things will smooth out for us. If you need comforting, then you can get it from her."

"I thought Captain Roark said she'd bite my nose off."

"That may be a slight exaggeration. As long as I tell her it's okay, she'll be fine, same as she was with Freddy."

Sobering and staring off into the distance as if visualizing her darling little boy, Zoe said, "It's him I'm most worried about."

"I thought you believed God was taking care of everything."

"I did, and I do. But I also believe He expects us to use the wits and weapons He's provided for us. Just because I know how to fly doesn't mean I'd carelessly go up without a parachute. That would be reckless."

"What about when you're on the ground?" Linc asked, eager for her answer.

He never expected her to look him straight in the eye and say, "When I'm down here, *you're* my parachute, Sergeant Colson. You and Star. I don't want to go anywhere without you until we figure out who is trying to destroy me."

FIFTEEN

The food at Carmen's was pleasing as usual, and so was the ambience. Linc reported their location and plans, then settled back to enjoy his meal.

She called me her parachute. He couldn't get that image out of his mind. A parachute slowed a jumper's descent, settled him gently on the ground and could be used again and again. But there was more to it than that, wasn't there? Zoe was counting on him to be her safety net, her ever-present, reliable guarantee that when all this was over, she'd survive the same way a parachute kept a jumper alive. Did she realize that the person in the harness had to know when to deploy an emergency chute? How to tuck and roll when making a hard landing? What to do if coming down in enemy territory?

Linc doubted she had made that detailed a comparison when she'd complimented him. That was just as well. As much as he wanted to be everything she needed, he knew that was impossible. So when had the pretty sergeant gone from being an assignment to something more? The change was in his outlook. In the way he perceived both her and their companionship. What had once been a job was now more than a pleasure, more than his duty. It was as if their lives had been joined by circumstances with the glue of compassion, perhaps even budding love.

Love? Linc looked across the table at her and found her studying him, as well. Hoping to seem nonchalant, he smiled and gestured with his fork. "Pretty good, huh? I love their lasagna."

Zoe mirrored his smile, but there was a poignancy in her eyes that made them glisten. Seconds later, she dropped her gaze to her plate and simply said, "Yes."

"Captain Roark says I may be able to take Star home with me tonight. Tomorrow at the latest."

"Good."

"Sergeant James is going to assign one of our female Security Forces members to your watch tonight. If I were you, I'd invite her in and let her crash on the couch. Her dog will alert if anybody approaches."

"Okay."

One-word answers were unlike Zoe, and her mental state had him worried. "Look. I know you say you're fine, but I'm not sure that's completely true. Talk to me. Tell me what's bothering you. I really do want to help."

She laid aside her fork and blotted her lips with a napkin before answering. "I know that. I just feel overwhelmed. So much has happened lately, and we have so few clues. It's as though I'm stuck in a flat spin at ten thousand feet and can't pull my aircraft out of it before I crash."

"You won't crash."

"How do you know? How can anybody be sure?"

Linc sighed. "Well, for one thing, we've got reports that your brother has been seen—"

"Stop." Teary-eyed, she held up a hand, palm toward him. "Stop calling him my brother, okay?"

"What should I call him?"

"I don't care. Call him Boyd or the Red Rose Killer or abbreviate it to RRK the way I've heard other law enforcement officers do. Just stop reminding me we're related. Please."

"All right. I'm sorry. I didn't think it would be a problem."

"Normally, it isn't." She sniffed and touched her napkin to her cheek where tears had begun to dampen it. "It's everything together. The attacks on me, the shooting I saw that left no trace, the—" Her eyes widened. "That's it! That's our answer."

"What is?"

"Fake blood. Like in my apartment. Your CSIs were using a blue light to look for the real thing in that warehouse bay. Nobody thought to check it for what that stuff in my apartment was made of."

"Whoa." Linc sat back in his chair. "You're right. I don't suppose there are traces of it left by now, even if there were drops in the first place, but I'll mention it to Captain Blackwood. Matter of fact, I'll do it right now. Wait here."

Zoe started to rise when he pulled out his cell and started for the door, so Linc repeated, "Wait here for me. I'll be right outside where I can see you."

He could tell she wanted to argue. To stay close to him. And although he knew that making the call in a crowded dining room wasn't smart, he was sorely tempted to do it anyway. Seeing Zoe's shoulders finally relax, he smiled back at her. "Thanks. This won't take a minute."

After wending his way between tables, Linc stepped outside as he was connecting. "Captain Blackwood.

This is Colson. I'm still with Sergeant Sullivan and in view of what was involved in this morning's incident at her apartment, we were wondering if that same artificial blood could have been used in the shooting she witnessed at the warehouse."

Silence on the line worried Linc until he heard his captain clear his throat. "You may be right. It'd be hard to tell at this point, though."

"It doesn't leave trace evidence?"

"Not that remains discernible. What we collected this morning was a homemade concoction instead of one of the professional brands the movies use. That kind lights up when we spray luminal. This stuff was made of food you'd find in most kitchen cupboards, as I said. Anything that landed on the ground outside was probably eaten by insects almost immediately."

"Hmm. Too bad. Zoe's going to be disappointed."

Blackwood's voice rose. "What did you say?"

"Sergeant Sullivan will be disappointed."

"No. You called her by her first name, Colson. I hope you remember that you are with her as a duty assignment."

"Yes, sir. Of course, Captain. It's just that—"

He was cut off. "No excuses. I know Master Sergeant James suggested that you befriend her, but that doesn't mean you should actually become personally involved. Is that clear?"

"Yes, sir. Crystal clear." *And almost totally unacceptable*, Linc added to himself. Personally involved? Oh, yeah. It was already too late to prevent that. So how was he going to obey orders and still guard Zoe to the degree necessary?

That was a good question. Too bad he didn't have

a good answer. Linc clenched his jaw muscles. He not only did not have a feasible idea, he didn't even have a poor one.

Turning on his heel, he straight-armed the restaurant door and returned to Zoe. *Yes, Zoe*, he affirmed. He'd have to take care to use her rank and last name when speaking to others, but in private, she was going to be Zoe.

Besides, he added, feeling his cheeks warming as their eyes met, he liked her, and Zoe was what he wanted to call her. What he would call her.

Linc smiled, rejoined her to report on the call and once again began to eat. The meal was cool and less appetizing than it had been but he was determined to finish so his companion would, too. She'd been picking at her food and he wanted her to keep up her energy.

"How about dessert?" Linc asked when she failed to follow his example.

Zoe shook her head and gave him a fond look that practically melted his heart. Why did he care so much? What in the world was wrong with him? Here he was, ready to defy a direct order and actually desiring chances to do so. That was more than stupid. It was insane.

Looking for a suitable diversion, Linc waved their waitress over.

"More sweet tea?" the young woman asked.

"Not for me. Zoe?"

"No, thanks." She sat back and pushed her plate away. "I'm finished."

"Then we'll have three slices of apple pie to go," he said. "And the bill."

"You remembered Freddy," Zoe said softly.

"Of course, I did. How could I forget Star's little buddy? I should have asked you if it was okay, though. Sorry."

"No need to apologize. It's more than okay," Zoe told him. "Way more. You'd be surprised how many adults overlook children."

"Your son's hard to overlook," Linc quipped. "He's a really special little guy."

The expression on Zoe's face made him wonder how he had upset her. She'd seemed a tad down in the dumps during their meal, but now she looked as if she might cry. Should he ask? Or should he go on as if he hadn't noticed?

Linc opted for the latter. He stood up and dropped a tip on the table. "We can settle up and get the pie at the register," he said. "Come on. It's time we checked in on Star again."

With a protective hand at her waist, he ushered her through the restaurant. The urge to keep her close was almost as strong as his determination to use her first name. Worse, he wasn't merely thinking of her as Zoe, he was seeing her as *his* Zoe. And there was no way he could talk himself out of it.

Seeing Star being her old self again made Zoe happy, but that was nothing compared to Linc's reaction. He was so overjoyed he was grinning from ear to ear. The exuberant dog obviously felt the same, because she was doing her version of the Texas two-step at his feet.

Zoe laughed. "I think she's happy to see you."

"Yeah." He tousled the recovered K-9's ears and laughed at her antics. "Something tells me she's ready to go back to work."

"Won't she be scared of being hurt again?" Zoe asked.

Captain Roark agreed. "Good point. How about a short retraining session? I'm sure we can find a volunteer to wear the bite sleeve."

"I'd rather send her after the real thing, but you're right. It would be a good idea. I'll check in with Caleb Streeter at the training center and set it up." He continued to pet the excited dog. "You sure she's ready for that much running this soon?"

"Absolutely." Roark smiled at Zoe. "And I owe you a puppy therapy session."

Although the idea appealed, she demurred. "Can I get a rain check? I'd rather come with my son and he's in day care during the week."

"Absolutely. Just let me know when you want to visit and I'll see that you and your son get the full tour."

"Thanks." Glancing at Linc, she couldn't help smiling. "I think they're glad to be back together."

"True. How are things going for you?"

She was touched that someone else was expressing concern. "Pretty good, considering. I still feel terrible that Star was hurt on my behalf."

"They're working dogs," Roark said. "We train for all branches of the military, as you probably know. Our K-9s are expected to do their jobs regardless of danger or injury."

"That sounds like the description of a human soldier."

Smiling, the vet agreed. "You're right. And we retire them after their working days are over, too. In fact, I'm waiting for one special case to be returned from overseas so I can check the dog's health and see if he's suitable for adoption, but there have been complications."

Linc straightened, still smiling broadly. "Sounds like the dog Isaac Goddard's been trying to adopt. Has there been any word?"

"Yes," Roark said. "Isaac was notified that Beacon had been cleared to return to the States, but there was an enemy attack on the base over there that damaged the kennels and the dog escaped. It's a crying shame. Isaac is having a really hard time dealing with the fact that Beacon may never be found and sent home."

"I understand exactly how he feels." Linc's hand was resting on Star's broad head.

Zoe smiled at both men. "I can see how important all the dogs are to you. I suppose it's inevitable that you'd get particularly attached to individual animals. I'm glad you get to adopt the retirees."

"Most of them qualify," Roark explained. "There's even a website where civilians can apply to adopt one of our dogs. There's a long waiting list, though, and strict requirements. The dog's handler gets first dibs."

She looked to Linc and Star. "Are you planning on keeping her if you can?"

"Absolutely. But it's going to be years before she's put out to pasture. We have a lot of work to do before that."

"Yes," Zoe said, "like capturing the Red Rose Killer and figuring out who has been making my life miserable." She heard a tiny gasp from behind her and turned. It was the vet tech who had taken care of Star when she first arrived, Airman Fielding.

Zoe easily identified with the fear she glimpsed in the young woman's eyes and offered solace. "Don't worry about the Red Rose Killer. I'm sure he'd have no reason to bother you, unless you dated him or crossed him somehow."

"I never met him," Fielding said. "Excuse me. I have patients to check."

Linc's brow was furrowed when Zoe looked to him and said, "She seems frightened."

Captain Roark agreed. "Rachel's always been kind of sensitive. Working here, surrounded by animals, is a perfect placement for her. Believe me, she's a lot calmer than she used to be."

"Good to hear," Zoe said. "If she were in one of my flight classes, I'm afraid she'd wash out quickly."

"Speaking of that, any word on when you can go back to work?" the vet asked.

"Nope. None." Smiling at Star, she added, "So for the time being, I'll be Star's volunteer sidekick. I can brush her and get her dog bones and…"

Linc was laughing when he held up a hand. "Whoa. That's my job. Sorry. How about you just try to stay out of trouble from now on and give us all a break?"

Eyes rolling, Zoe chuckled, too. "That, Sergeant Colson, is my fondest wish. From your mouth to God's ears, as they say here in the South."

Although he didn't stop smiling, he did say, "I doubt I have much influence on Him."

"You'd be surprised," Zoe countered. "God loves everybody who believes in Him. Even stubborn, hard-headed guys like you."

That made Roark laugh, too. "Look out, Colson. I think she's got you pegged."

Although Linc made a face at them both, Zoe thought she glimpsed a flicker of recognition, a spark of truth. She knew he didn't have to fully accept all his losses, in Afghanistan and before. He simply had to let go of his guilt and anger and hand it all over to his heavenly Father.

As I have to do regarding Boyd, she added to herself, knowing she was right. It wasn't the understanding she lacked, it was the will to act, the strength to forgive. And the faith to trust so completely that she was able to release her wounded spirit into the care of a loving God.

That wasn't the same as worshipping on Sunday morning. It went much, much deeper.

SIXTEEN

"I need to step next door and check in with my bosses before we do anything else," Linc said.

Zoe didn't mind. She shrugged and smiled. "Fine with me. As you can see, I'm free."

He started off, Star at his side, and Zoe followed. "So, what are you planning for later?"

"Don't know yet. We have several options. I want to ask if the techs found any traces of syrup on the floor of the warehouse."

"Unlikely, I'm afraid."

"Probably. But I asked them to look just the same."

"Thanks. I can't believe I fell for the ruse." She kept walking but paused the conversation before adding, "If it really was a trick."

"Let's assume it was. That leaves us with fewer suspects."

"How so?"

"If the same theatrical blood was used, that will combine two of the incidents."

"Makes sense." She followed Linc and Star to Captain Blackwood's open office door. Linc knocked on the jamb.

Justin Blackwood stood behind his desk and Zoe saluted, as did Linc.

"I see Star is back in service. Good to know."

"Yes, sir. Since Sergeant Sullivan is free to move around the base, I wondered if you had anything we might handle together."

"Such as?"

Zoe could tell Blackwood wasn't thrilled with Linc's suggestion, but as far as she was concerned, it made perfect sense. She cleared her throat. "Excuse me, sir. If I may? Since the Red Rose Killer is very familiar to me, it makes sense to send me out in the field with one of your Security people. My chances of spotting him in a crowd are far better than anyone else's."

The captain nodded slightly, acting as if he was at least considering her views. "There is some logic to your suggestion, Sullivan. I assume that wherever you go you're on alert for any sign of your brother."

Zoe tried not to cringe at the familial reference. "Yes, sir. The RRK is always on my mind. So is whoever has been harassing me. I don't think my case is related to the serial killings. At least I hope it isn't."

Blackwood shuffled papers on his desk and selected one. "I have a report from Yvette Crenville. She's accusing Jim Ahern of bothering her again."

"Yes, sir," Linc said. "We visited him at work at the airfield earlier today."

"And?"

"He seems pretty full of himself but mostly hot air," Linc replied. "What I'd like to do is check on some of the possible suspects in Sergeant Sullivan's repeated attacks. There have been too many to chalk them up to chance."

"Agreed. Having a motive would help. Any ideas, Sergeant?" he asked, giving Zoe a piercing look.

"Not really, sir. Sergeant Colson and I made a list. Once we've compared duty assignments to the times of the incidents, we should be able to eliminate quite a few suspects."

"Then get to it. I'll bring in someone to assist you with the computer details if you want." The captain glanced at another list. "Airman McNally is available." He keyed his intercom. "Send McNally to my office."

Zoe didn't want her problems spread all over the base due to additional exposure, so she gently objected to the suggestion. "I think Colson and I can handle it by ourselves, sir. Once we have access to individual records, it should be easy."

A sharp knock against the open door caused Zoe to pivot. The airman was not only a woman, she was young, lithe and had her hair pulled tightly back into a coil, the same way Zoe wore hers when she was working. That wasn't what made Zoe take a quick involuntary breath however. It was the airman's hair color. McNally was a redhead!

Had Linc made the connection yet? Zoe wondered. If he gave in and let his captain assign this woman to their project, there was no telling what might happen. Yes, she was undoubtedly not the only female on base who had red hair. But the coincidence was bothersome.

Swaying slightly, Zoe felt Linc's hand at her back, his touch barely there yet supportive. She chanced a sidelong glance and saw that their minds were in sync. Raising her chin a mere millimeter and hoping no one but Linc noticed, she turned the motion into a slow, purposeful nod. The narrowing of his eyes indicated comprehension.

"Thank you anyway, Captain," he said. "Sullivan and I can manage."

"Then you're excused," Blackwood told the assistant.

"One thing before I go, sir?" McNally waited.

Although the redheaded airman seemed to be ignoring her, Zoe was certain she was picking up bad vibes. Either that or her overactive imagination was blaming an innocent party, which was also possible.

Blackwood nodded. "Go ahead."

"It's that blogger, sir. He's already posted info about the attack on Sergeant Colson's dog and reported that the K-9 is sidelined."

Meaning everybody at CAFB is already privy to my problems, Zoe thought, chagrined. *Terrific.*

Obviously displeased, Blackwood clenched his jaw and his fists. "All right. Get the techs on it again ASAP. We have enough internal stress without adding some idiot with a computer and too much time on his hands."

"Yes, sir." McNally saluted and left.

The captain jotted down a note and handed it to Linc. "Here's today's password. You can use Sergeant James's office if it's free. If not, I'll get you access somewhere else. I don't want to learn that either of you has opened files belonging to any personnel other than the ones you're investigating. Is that clear?"

Linc saluted. "Yes, sir. Very clear."

Mirroring Linc's salute, Zoe followed him into the hallway and checked to see that they were alone before she said, "What do you think? Could that be her?"

"It could. You weren't able to give a very detailed description of the woman in the warehouse. What makes you think it was McNally?"

"I don't know, exactly. Maybe the way she moved or her build, not to mention that hair."

"There's something else," Linc said, pulling her closer to his side and bending to speak more privately. "The way she looked at you when you weren't paying attention. I think I saw recognition. Had you met her anywhere before?"

"Not to my knowledge. Maybe we should do a little extra investigating while we're at it."

"I don't know. You heard the captain."

"I did. So let's start with my list and leave our new suspect for last, just in case we get shut out."

Linc's sly grin and the purposeful way he led her to the empty office they were supposed to use lifted Zoe's spirits immensely. Not only was he on her side, they had begun to agree more often than not. Teamwork was far better than working at odds and she had high hopes that they would soon solve at least one of the mysteries they faced.

Star accompanied them down the hallway and into the office of Master Sergeant James. Zoe could tell that the faithful K-9 was more at ease than both her or Linc. When he closed the door behind them her tension rose. They were all alone. And he had been acting awfully proprietary of late. It was easy to imagine herself back in his embrace, perhaps even kissed. Although, after making a fool of herself once, she wasn't about to try to instigate anything romantic.

"Don't worry," Linc assured her. "You're safe with me. I promise to be the perfect gentleman."

A daring side of Zoe's personality that she rarely acknowledged emerged, and she whispered, "That's what

I'm afraid of," before she could change her mind. Linc's startled expression was actually amusing.

"What did you say?"

"Never mind. Forget it."

Instead, he approached slowly and took her hand. "You're trembling."

"Too much coffee."

"Liar."

What could she say? How could she take back her revealing remark? Moreover, did she want to? Especially when he was standing so close, and she saw the glow in his darkening, expressive green eyes.

Instead of a rebuttal, Zoe kept her gaze locked with his. Her lips trembled. Her heart was about to pound out of her chest. And the air in the small office must have been used up because she couldn't seem to take a deep enough breath to keep her comfortable.

Linc slipped one finger beneath her chin and leaned closer. "I am probably going to be sorry for this," he said quietly against her cheek before turning his head just enough and giving her the kiss she had been dreaming of.

Her shaky equilibrium wasn't strong enough to correct the sway his nearness provoked, so she slipped both arms around his waist. When he completed the embrace and pulled her to him to deepen their kiss, Zoe closed her eyes and surrendered. Utterly. Completely. Trusting him with an intensity she had always assumed was impossible for her.

Tears threatened as she realized what he had said. Well, he might be sorry for kissing her, but as far as Zoe was concerned, this was the best part of her whole day. Maybe of her whole life.

Yeah. The best.

* * *

Linc became oblivious to anything around them. His entire focus was on Zoe. On the sweet smell of her hair. The way she fit so perfectly in his arms. And that kiss.

He was no kid. He'd kissed women before. And he'd enjoyed it. A lot. But this was different. When his mind tried to put his feelings into words, it failed. Their closeness was too perfect. Too emotional. Too amazing to be explained.

That was what finally brought him to his senses. Zoe wasn't the only one breathless when he let her go and set her away by gently cupping her shoulders. Oh, man, he was in trouble. Deep trouble. This was no simple crush, at least not on his part. He wondered if her responses to him had been because she felt their connection as strongly as he did or because she'd been so frightened lately and had latched onto him as a port in a storm. After all, she had compared him to a parachute. If that was all he was to her, then he was probably going to get his heart broken. Big time.

Linc managed a smile. "I told you we were going to be sorry."

"We? Personally, I liked it."

"That's it? You liked it?"

She grinned up at him, her cheeks rosy, her eyes glistening. Linc cupped her cheeks. "I liked it, too."

"Good." She sniffled.

"If you expect me to be poetic about it, you're going to have to give me time to gather my wits. You scattered them really well just now." He eyed the desk. Star had made herself at home in the kneehole and was starting to snore. "Do you think you're up to starting our search or do you need a few more minutes?"

"If you could give me a year, it probably wouldn't be long enough," Zoe quipped. Squaring her shoulders, she said, "Come on. Let's get to digging. We don't know how long we'll have before Sergeant James wants his office back."

Linc agreed. "I'm glad he didn't walk in a few minutes ago."

"Me, too. He might have reassigned you and spoiled everything."

"We'd still have been stationed on the same base." Linc circled the desk, pulled up the swivel chair and checked the password Blackwood had given him.

Standing behind him, Zoe rested a hand on his shoulder and watched the monitor. He knew she didn't mean to be distracting but after that extraordinary kiss, even the simple touch of her hand on his uniform was enough to drive him crazy.

His fingers stopped typing. All movement ceased.

Zoe's hand remained where it was. "What's wrong?"

"You are," Linc admitted ruefully. "I'm afraid I can't think straight when you're so close."

"That's too bad," she said, pulling away and choosing a nearby chair.

When Linc looked over at her, she was grinning from ear to ear. Already uneasy, he scowled. "What?"

"Nothing." She crossed her jeans-clad legs and held out a hand. "Give me the list and I'll read you the names from way over here. Did I go far enough?"

"It's not funny," he insisted.

Zoe sobered and took the list from him. "I know. It just struck me as hilarious that the two of us were forced together when we both hate the idea of marriage."

"Whoa! Who said anything about *that*?"

"Nobody. Just thinking aloud. I didn't mean to scare the stripes off you, Sergeant Colson."

Her nonchalant shrug seemed innocent enough, but Linc wasn't convinced. One kiss and already she was hearing wedding bells. Well, that wasn't going to happen. Not with him. Sure, Zoe was attractive. And that kiss had shaken him all the way to the waffled soles of his combat boots. But he'd promised himself a long time ago that one, the influence of his dysfunctional family was nothing he wanted to pass on to future generations, and two, he didn't deserve marital bliss when his buddies' wives and girlfriends had buried their dreams with their mates.

Uh-uh. Linc Colson was staying single. He might be too romantic for his own good, but he knew where to draw the line. Lifelong penance for his errors in judgment was necessary. There was no escape from his past, nor was he looking for one.

SEVENTEEN

By the time Linc had completed his survey and cut the list down to the likely suspects, Zoe's neck was in knots and her head throbbed. She knew why. Spending all this time with him was very trying. If he hadn't been on duty, it might have been different, although she doubted it.

Standing, she stretched. "I should go get Freddy soon."

"Right. We will. The boy comes first. We don't want him to be worried about you."

We? Zoe wondered if noticing every little nuance of Linc's behavior was something new or if she had been doing it all along and had overlooked her own interest. Until now. Moreover, did he realize he had begun referring to them as a couple? Whatever. She certainly wasn't going to be the one to point it out.

One concern she was going to mention however, was the safety of her beloved child. "Do you think, considering everything that's happened, that I should send Freddy away?"

Linc whirled, scowling. "What brought that on?"

"Reality," she said flatly. "He's all I have. I love him so much it hurts. There must be some way to protect him."

"Better than I can, you mean." It wasn't a question.

"I didn't say that." She was adamant. "But you can't be around all the time. And at night, when he's home with me, you're not there at all. Somebody else is."

"With a K-9 partner."

"I know, I know. And that is a plus. But those guards keep changing. I never know who's going to show up. When I see you, it's very reassuring."

"Thanks, I think." He drew his fingers and thumb down the sides of his jaw, meeting at the point of his chin. "I suppose it's possible I could convince Sergeant James to switch my assignment to the overnight shift, but that may be a bad idea."

"Why? If you're still worried about rumors about being in my apartment, I assure you, I trust you completely. Besides, Freddy's there. I can let him bunk with me and you can have his room."

Linc held up both hands, palms out. "Whoa. Is that where your other night watchmen sleep?"

"Well, no. I've offered something more comfortable, but they've all turned me down."

"As they should have," Linc said forcefully.

"You don't have to raise your voice. I'm the victim here, remember? I'm just worried about protecting my son the best way possible. As I said, maybe I should send him away."

"Where? Where would you send him? You've already told me your family is unfit. What about the Flints, John's parents? Would they take him in? He is their grandson."

"Not one they choose to claim. They disowned me and mine long ago after I reported John's crimes. They never did believe he could be guilty of espionage and insisted I had framed him." She sighed. "I think they suspect me of being behind the accident that killed him, too."

"Sad. They're missing out on meeting a great kid."

Linc's praise restored Zoe's smile and lifted her spirits until he added, "You can't leave him with Maisy overnight. Not with her father being one of the RRK's victims."

Zoe knew he was right. Maisy's father, Chief Master Sergeant Clint Lockwood, had been one of her brother's first victims on CAFB.

She made a face. "*Him* again." She began to pace. "You have no idea how much I wish I had been an only child."

He chuckled wryly. "I used to, too, until my sister, Georgia, became an adult. Now we just fight over which branch of the service is the best, hers or mine."

"She's an army major, right?"

"You have a good memory. Yes. A career officer."

"What does she do? I mean, what's her specialty?" Zoe hoped Linc didn't think she was just making conversation. She truly wanted to know.

"Diplomacy, if you can believe it." He laughed lightly. "We are definitely not alike."

"Oh, I don't know. I've seen you handle lots of touchy situations since you've been assigned to me. You're an impressive negotiator, too."

"Yeah, well. I've made some mistakes."

Like kissing me? she wondered. Rather than ask and chance confirmation, Zoe let it pass. "We all make mistakes," she said. "Some more than others. Take my—take the Red Rose Killer. He had every opportunity to turn his life around and refused."

"Don't beat yourself up about it," Linc said. "The

same goes for lots of criminals, including my own father. They seem oblivious to the harm they're leaving in their wake and the people they're disappointing."

"I suspect they just don't care, for the most part," Zoe suggested. "I mean, look at the two of us. We could be offered any reward on earth and it wouldn't be enough to turn us against our country."

"You're right."

"Of course, I am, as I've proved before. I've come to another conclusion, too. In spite of the possibility that the RRK has likely been on the base, I don't think my problems can be pinned on him no matter how we twist the clues. It just isn't his MO."

"Listen to you," Linc said with a low chuckle, "sounding like a professional cop."

"I get bored and watch a lot of TV after Freddy's in bed. Well? Do you agree or are you still including you-know-who among your suspects?"

"No. I'm convinced it's somebody else who has it in for you."

"What about the blood?"

"The blood that wasn't real? The shooting that didn't happen? Missing babysitting money? A car with a useless bomb?"

Zoe gasped. "What bomb?"

"I guess I forgot to tell you."

"Yeah, I guess." Arms folded across her chest, she struck a formidable looking pose. "Talk."

"Nick Donovan's bomb sniffer didn't react and the ordnance people didn't see anything under the chassis. But when they looked in the gas tank, they found a cell phone wired to what looked like a really thin pipe bomb.

According to them, there was no way the thing would have detonated after soaking in gasoline for so long."

"Hold on." Her eyebrows knit together. "What about sooner? Suppose I had ignored your warning and driven?"

"That's unknown." Linc held up a hand. "Don't get excited. Whoever put the device in your tank was a doofus when it comes to ordnance. Believe me, I've dealt with serious bomb makers, and they don't fool around with untried methods."

The darkness in his gaze and the hurt in his tone were enough to stop her from giving voice to the questions that rose in her mind. Just what kind of experience with bombs had he had? She changed the subject. "Never mind that now. What are we going to do about taking care of Freddy?"

"I thought I'd request permission to crash in my car outside your apartment building while the regular guard takes inside duty as usual."

"Oh." That solution, while logical, did not include her personal preferences. How could she express them without making Linc think she was pursuing him? Why, oh, why, had she let herself get carried away making jokes and bringing up the subject of marriage, particularly after he'd told her how he felt regarding a lifelong commitment?

Zoe's mind provided no ready answer. There was no way to go back in time and retract her faux pas. Therefore, she reasoned, the best plan for going forward was to agree with Linc's ideas and bend her will to his. His being parked outside was more sensible and far less stressful—for both of them. Zoe didn't know about Linc, but her heart beat faster the instant she dared relive even the most innocent moments of their embrace. And that fantastic kiss!

Thousands of romance novels had been written about such things. Until then, she had assumed a reaction like the one she'd had while in his arms was a figment of an author's creative imagination. Well, no more. She and Linc had ignited a forest fire, and he was trying to put it out with the equivalent of a teaspoon of water, when what they should have been doing was turning from each other and running in opposite directions as fast as they could.

Only he would never abandon his duty, would he? And there was nowhere she could go, no way she could hope to safely escape both her antagonist and the dedicated Security Forces man who was trying to protect her. She was in the air force. She went where she was told.

Besides, she admitted with a dose of self-criticism, she was not going to purposely flee from the only person who had made her feel totally secure in more years than she could count.

Forcing a smile, she slipped her thumbs into the front pockets of her jeans, struck a casual pose and said, "Whatever you decide is fine with me. C'mon. Let's go get Freddy."

In Linc's mind, he had wandered empty-handed into a swamp filled with hungry alligators. Or perhaps barefoot into a cave of venomous snakes. Whatever the inane analogy, he was up to his neck in trouble with a capital *Z* for *Zoe*.

I can't possibly have fallen for her, he told himself. That would be disastrous. Despite her joking manner, he suspected she'd been serious when she'd vowed to never remarry. That was fine with him. Wasn't it? If so, then why was his gut tying in knots every time he saw her threatened or remembered the times she'd been inches from injury?

Because I'm an idiot, he replied. What good was it to plan his career, his life, if he let a pretty face distract him from reaching his goals?

What he could do was request he be relieved of duty regarding Sergeant Sullivan altogether. The thought had briefly crossed his mind in the past but certainly not lately. No. He was going to stick it out and prove to himself that he could rise above emotion and that he was in total control, mind and body. Thankfully, rigid self-discipline would keep his actions in line. His errant thoughts were a very different story.

He'd been to church often enough to recall Scripture insisting that a wrong thought was the same as the deed. They sure didn't feel the same to Linc. And there lay the conundrum. His feelings had taken control and were running rampant, urging him to do or say something he knew would bring pain to himself and to Zoe. Linc clenched his jaw. *Not to mention Freddy.*

The little guy deserved a better father than he could ever hope to be. If Zoe didn't realize that, maybe it was time to remind her.

Linc led the way to his car, put Star into the rear and held a front door for Zoe. As she passed close by to slip into the SUV, he caught a whiff of her shampoo. She smelled like flowers. Her hair was down again, brushing against her shoulders in silky light brown waves. And those expressive eyes. He knew better than to dwell on her hazel gaze because every time he did, it became more difficult to look away.

He climbed behind the wheel and gripped it hard. Out of the corner of his right eye, he could see her peering over at him, so he said the first thing that came to mind. "Do you have all the groceries and housekeeping supplies you need? If not, we should stop at the BX before we pick up Freddy."

"I'm good. I try to stock extras so I don't have to shop too often. I hate wasting time."

"A woman who doesn't like to shop? Now, that is something for the newspapers."

"Well, you could contact Heidi Jenks."

"Not likely. There's a strong suspicion she may be our mysterious blogger. I sure don't want to feed her any more information, even accidentally, and see it turn up on everybody's computers."

"You mean like the time that blog listed the RRK's supposed romantic interests? It wasn't only the women who had already got a red rose and a warning note. There were others, too."

"I know. I visited Jolie Potter, the scientist who works in our biomedical lab. All she recalled was a few dates and Boyd dumping her because he claimed she was too smart. I also spoke to Munitions Specialist Lara Dennie. She admitted to having had a crush on him but said she'd dodged a bullet when he'd ignored her. Those women were both on a classified list that only authorized personnel should have had access to."

"Then how would Lieutenant Jenks...?"

"Unknown. Just like so many other facets of what's been going on around here." He made the turn onto the side road leading to the preschool. Not only did Zoe perk up when the building came in sight, so did Star.

Linc gave a low chuckle. "I think my K-9 is glad we're picking up her little buddy. Look at her."

"I see." Zoe's laugh carried tones of fondness for the dog that would have surprised Linc coming from anyone else. "It's a pleasure to have her around, particularly when her favorite person is Freddy."

"Whoa." Linc had to grin. "I am supposed to be the one and only person Star is interested in. I told you not to spoil her by making her too social."

"Phooey. I didn't make her anything. You and I both know she had a soft side all along. Just because she wags that stubby tail more when Freddy and I are around is no reason to blame us."

"Oh, no?"

"No." Zoe pointed to the curb. "Just pull over right here and I'll run in to get him."

"We'll come with you."

She didn't say it, but he saw the objection in her eyes and body language. She obviously did not want an escort, although why was puzzling. She had just told him she wanted him close, yet she was acting as if he'd insulted her. "What?" he asked.

Zoe was shaking her head the way a trainer did when a particularly dense canine didn't pick up instruction quickly enough. "It's perfectly safe here. You'll be in the car and your dog will alert if anything's wrong." She pushed open the passenger door and hopped out. "Stand by, Sergeant. I'll be right back."

Because he had scanned the approach and the yard already, Linc felt reasonably certain Zoe would be fine. After all, he hadn't been assigned to become her Siamese twin, he'd merely been told to keep watch and try to convince her to trust him.

Well, mission accomplished, he thought cynically. Sergeant Sullivan trusted him implicitly. Remembering that kiss, he wondered if that was more of a problem than if she had held him at arm's length.

Linc saw her climb the front steps and knock. It took several seconds for the door to open and Zoe to be admitted. Then it shut tight. Good. The women inside were properly protecting their charges. It was a shame they had to worry so much but that was better than being too lax.

Moving back and forth in the seat behind him, Star was acting anxious. "Settle down, girl. She'll be back soon."

The dog continued to fidget. When she let out one of her impressive rottweiler barks, Linc took her seriously. Just because he hadn't seen or sensed a problem didn't mean Star was wrong.

He stepped out of the SUV, fastened a lead on his K-9 partner and gave her the command to jump down. She took off so fast and pulled so hard that Linc almost lost his footing. Her nose was to the ground now, the hackles on the back of her neck and shoulders bristling. He might not know what she was after but as long as Star did, Linc was going to let her search.

They crossed a sparse lawn, rounded the preschool and made the corner, then slowed. Star froze as if she were a hunting dog, signaling a hidden pheasant. She sniffed the air. Then the bare dirt. A fenced play area stopped them from continuing right next to the building, so Linc urged his dog to backtrack. She didn't refuse, but he could tell she wasn't happy about the redirection.

A child's laughter reached them both. Star began to strain. Linc kept her controlled so she wouldn't race around to the front and flatten some poor kid with her enthusiasm, probably Freddy. "Easy, Star. Heel."

The look the K-9 gave him was so full of frustration and angst it was almost comical. She'd probably led him to the play area because she knew children had recently been out there and was disappointed when he'd pulled her away.

A female voice called, "Linc? Sergeant Colson?"

Zoe. He was about to answer when her words morphed into a scream.

With every nerve firing and every muscle taut, Linc raced back toward his vehicle. Zoe! Someone wearing a jumpsuit and a baseball cap had hold of her and was grappling for control while brave little Freddy pounded tiny fists against the man's legs.

Linc drew his gun and shouted, "Security! Hands up."

EIGHTEEN

Zoe fought for her child with all her strength, all her heart, every maternal instinct she had. Nobody was going to harm her little boy as long as she had breath in her body.

The man's hold tightened, pinning her arms so she couldn't get a good swing at him. Remembering her training, she bent lower and tried to use his own momentum to pitch him over her head. Instead, she found herself hurtling toward the ground when he suddenly released her.

Everything was happening so fast that the surrounding scene was a blur. A male shouting, a dog barking and Freddy… The moment Zoe regained her senses enough to act she reached for her beloved child. Freddy leaped into her open arms with such force he knocked her backward. Gasping, she pulled him close and showered kisses all over his tear-streaked face.

Feet wearing combat boots thundered past. "Linc?"

There was no immediate answer. It had to be him. He had not waited for her in the car the way he'd promised, yet he must have remained close by. She knew he'd never have abandoned her. Not in a million years. So where was he?

Fierce barking and growling at the side of the house

was her answer. *Star!* That was the dark-colored blur she'd seen passing as she fell. The K-9 was in attack mode. Hopefully, this time Linc was there to back her up.

Freddy began struggling to free himself. "Too tight, Mama."

"I'm sorry, honey." Zoe managed to get to her feet without letting go of the boy's hand. As soon as she was certain she was stable, she scooped him up. "I was so worried about you. Why didn't you run away like we practiced?"

The child pouted. "Uh-uh. He was hurting you."

Zoe buried her face against his little neck and fought back tears. "I understand. I'm not mad, Freddy. Honest, I'm not. I know you were doing what you thought was right."

Assuming Linc had captured her attacker, Zoe was slack jawed when he and Star returned alone. The dog seemed okay this time, but Linc's beret was missing and he was rubbing the back of his head.

"Linc? Are you hurt?"

"Mostly my pride," he said gruffly. "Star had him until somebody conked me in the head and she let go to come check me."

"Is she supposed to do that?"

"No." He cast a disparaging glance at his dog. "We'll be doing some retraining ASAP." Then he turned back to Zoe. "I'm sorry we didn't apprehend the suspect. This is the most physical attack he's made on you so far."

Zoe was kneading her neck. "Yeah. Tell me about it." She watched as Linc crouched to examine his dog, presumably checking for unseen injuries. "What's she chewing on?"

Linc commanded the K-9 to release. She placed a soggy piece of fabric in his outstretched hand. He stood and displayed it in his palm. "What does that look like to you?"

"Part of a dark blue jumpsuit like our mechanics sometimes wear."

"Exactly." Linc tucked the scrap into a plastic evidence baggie. "As chewed as this is, I doubt the lab can isolate DNA, but our next stop is going to be the airfield. I want to see who's missing a piece of his south end."

"Might Star have made him bleed?" Zoe wasn't cowed when Linc gave her a quizzical look, so she added, "I hope so."

"I see your spirit isn't harmed. That's good, because we're now searching for two assailants—the one who grabbed you just now and the person who hit me over the head from behind."

"Two?" She hadn't progressed that far in her reasoning, but now it registered. "Of course. Remember the warehouse? There were two involved there, too. A man and a woman. Maybe she's still working with him."

"Maybe." Linc gave her a lopsided smile. "Don't stress that notion in your debriefing, okay? I'll report it, but I'd just as soon the other members of my unit didn't start teasing me about being taken down by a female."

Zoe huffed. "Why not? We can swing a baseball bat as well as anybody. Stop acting so macho and admit it."

That brought a chuckle and another exploration of the knot on his head. "Granted. But in this case, she either went easy on me or didn't have a man's strength, because I don't think I have a concussion."

"Maybe she didn't intend to kill you."

"Let's hope not," Linc replied. "The last thing the base needs is another bona fide killer roaming the streets."

* * *

Zoe argued that she didn't need a visit to the ER but went along after Linc convinced her by agreeing to be checked out, as well. As soon as they were given clean bills of health, he suggested they stop at an ice-cream parlor to buy Freddy a cone.

Zoe wiped the drippings off her son's chin as she spoke. "So, what are they planning to do for a guard at my place tonight?"

"My captain is considering letting me hang around, if that's what you mean," Linc replied. "You'll still have someone else watching who is actually assigned."

"Good."

The bell over the shop door jingled and drew his attention. "Well, what do you know." He stood. "Excuse me for a second?"

"Sure. I'll wait here with Mr. Sticky."

Grinning, Linc stepped forward and saluted. "Lieutenant Webb. I thought you'd be off enjoying a well-earned vacation by now."

Ethan Webb shook Linc's hand vigorously. "So did I. My time off was delayed because my K-9 and I were needed here at Canyon." He lowered his voice. "Now there are more reports of sightings of the Red Rose Killer at Baylor Marine Base."

"More?"

"Yes." He urged Linc aside so the two friends could speak privately. "Lieutenant Colonel Masters over at Baylor used to be my father-in-law, as you know, and he's asking for me. Insisting, really."

"Do you think Jillian is behind his request?"

Ethan's grimace at the mention of his ex-wife was fleeting yet telling. "Possibly. She's impossible to predict. I'd hoped she was done causing me trouble when she divorced me."

"Maybe she is. Her father may just be taking advantage of his high rank to bring in outside help he trusts. What I don't get is why he's poaching on our turf when he's got a base full of marines."

"I think it's because of my K-9. He wants Titus. Besides, Jillian has always got whatever Jillian wants. That's a big reason our marriage failed. I had no idea she was so spoiled when I proposed."

Glancing back at the small round table where Zoe and Freddy sat, Linc gestured. "Why don't you take a load off and join us? It's safe to talk about personal stuff in front of Zoe."

"Thanks, but I have to be going." Ethan grinned. "You finally settling down, Colson? That's a huge surprise."

"It's not what it looks like," Linc insisted. "I've been assigned to guard the sergeant and her son."

"Looks pretty cozy to me." Ethan hesitated. "Don't mention anything about Jillian, okay? Whatever Colonel Masters wants may work itself out after I've spoken to him in person. Boyd Sullivan may not actually be at Baylor right now, even if Jillian did get the customary red rose and warning note."

"Sure. No problem. How's Titus?"

"Fine," Ethan told him. "You and Star still good?"

"Absolutely. She's out in the car with the air running to keep her comfortable. We'd all be out there if she wasn't so fond of that kid—and ice cream."

The lieutenant chuckled and clapped Linc on the shoulder. "You know what they say, Colson. When in doubt, trust your K-9."

"Those two have more than won over Star. If I'm not careful, they'll turn her into a useless lap dog." He shook his friend's hand once again. "Take care. And keep your defenses up around your ex. Don't let a woman get to you."

Ethan eyed the table and smiled broadly. "Same to you, buddy."

Thankfully, Zoe hadn't run out of napkins by the time Linc returned. "All done," she said. "Time to order mine to go."

"I didn't understand why you wanted to wait to eat yours until I saw Freddy with that cone. Yuck."

"Licking drips takes practice when you're only three. So who was the officer?"

"An old friend who handles Titus, a German short-haired pointer."

"Doesn't sound like an attack breed," Zoe said.

"Titus isn't. He's been used for patrol and is a great cadaver dog. Ethan's back from combat and due for some R & R. Unfortunately, he may be sent to Baylor Marine Base because of possible sightings of…"

"Oh, brother." She made a face. "Literally. I hope your friend gets his time off soon. I'm sure he deserves it. That sounds like an awful job to train for."

"I wouldn't want it," Linc admitted. He smiled down on her and she warmed considerably. "Now, for our ice-cream cones. What flavor for you?"

"One scoop of cherry chocolate walnut, thanks. What are you having?"

"Plain vanilla. I don't like to ruin good ice cream by loading it up with other flavors."

Freddy clapped his sticky hands. "I love 'nilla."

"You and me both, kid," Linc said with a grin before walking away. Zoe was positive she'd glimpsed a tenderness in his eyes when he'd smiled down at her son. And, truth be told, she sometimes imagined the same fond expression settling on her. Whether that was true or not, she felt good when Linc smiled at her. More than good, actually. His approval, spoken or implied, gave her spirits a boost like the afterburner on a jet. Being around him was so wonderful, so sweet, so…

"Fool," Zoe muttered to herself, pulling a face. She was doing it again. Kidding herself by imagining a happy future with the wrong man.

But was he wrong? Never mind his insistence that he intended to stay single. What if he was considering changing his mind? What if he was starting to feel as much affection toward her as she was feeling for him?

"That'll be the day," she mumbled, using a glass of water to dampen a fresh napkin and wipe Freddy's hands some more.

The deep voice behind her made her jump so badly she nearly tipped over the glass. "What will be the day?"

Linc was back with their cones. In a flash, Zoe tried to recall how much she had actually uttered aloud and how much had been silent thought. She looked up to study him. Since he didn't seem upset, she figured she was safe.

"Um, when my son can eat without taking a bath in it."

"He does pretty well on pizza."

"Only because I cut it up for him." She reached for her treat. "Is this mine?"

"Yup. And this is mine." As he began to lick the cone, Zoe decided it was best if she looked away. Everything

Linc did, every word he spoke, every shadow of a smile he displayed sent her heart racing and made her hands tremble. Had he asked what was bothering her, she intended to blame her unrest on her stalker. That would be partially true. But it wasn't an adversary who had her nerves in knots and filled her stomach with butterflies. It was her new friend. Her protector. The one man she had finally decided wasn't half bad.

That conclusion made her grin. Rather than giggle, she started to eat. The ice cream was delicious. "Mmm."

"Glad you like it," Linc said. "For a minute there, you looked so strange I was afraid I'd got the wrong flavor."

Zoe hid behind the cone and bided her time by systematically licking all the way around. "No problem. It's wonderful."

What drew her attention back to Linc was not his words or actions; it was the lack of either. Instead of continuing to eat, he had stopped and was staring across the table at her. There was the tender look again. She wasn't imagining it. She couldn't be. He wasn't smiling. He wasn't frowning. But his concentration was so complete, so absolute, she almost shivered.

"Yeah," he finally said, continuing to have eyes only for her, while patrons of the ice-cream parlor came and went past their table and Freddy slapped his hands on it as if playing a drum.

Zoe held her breath, hoping against hope that Linc was ready to express his personal feelings, to perhaps say something romantic. Judging by his fond expression, it was certainly a possibility.

She was left guessing what he had meant when he stared into her wide eyes, smiled and quietly said, "Wonderful."

If they had not been surrounded by a crowd and accompanied by her lovable but nosy child, she might have asked for clarification.

Oh, sure, and have Linc tell me he was talking about the ice cream? No way. There was no reason to chance making a fool of herself. There would be plenty of time to stick her foot in her mouth again, as she had when she'd mentioned marriage and scared him silly. After all, they hadn't even dated, let alone admitted serious intentions.

Except that we've already spent more hours together than some couples have managed after months of dating, particularly those in the military, she added to herself. It was possible to fall in love, even when a significant other was stationed half a world away, wasn't it?

Suppose that was Linc's problem? Suppose the beautiful woman who he'd admitted had betrayed him still held a place in his heart? Could his reticence be caused by that? Did Zoe have a rival who had achieved special status merely because she was unattainable?

Further thought led her to decide against that theory. Linc was a patriot, a straight shooter, an honorable man who would never be able to forgive someone who had betrayed his comrades-in-arms and threatened the well-being of his homeland.

That thought led her directly to John Flint. She had revealed his treason as soon as she'd learned of it. Was that enough for Linc to see her as the red-blooded American that she was? Or did he paint her with the same brush of evil that some of her fellow airmen had?

Chagrined, Zoe almost wished Linc's hang-up, if he had one, would be her first marriage, because that was over. John Flint was no more. Her familial connection to her brother, however, would never go away, and she wondered if her reputation would always be tied to his, however tenuously.

Deciding to redirect her own thoughts and Linc's, Zoe asked a question she thought was fairly innocuous. "What's the latest on that pesky blogger? Any success finding him?"

Her companion's negative expression surprised her. She frowned. "What are you not telling me?"

Linc shook his head. "Not important."

"It is if it bothers you," she countered.

"I take it you haven't looked." Using his phone to open to the web, Linc passed it to her. "See for yourself."

Zoe peered at the small screen. "This blames everything Boyd did on me. How dare they!"

"Doesn't matter. We know you're innocent."

"We? You and I, maybe, but not the rest of the base." She passed the phone back to Linc. "I've seen enough."

"Okay. Sorry, but you did ask." Zoe saw him briefly glance at the screen before raising it to read more carefully.

"What's the matter? More accusations?"

"Not exactly. I paged down, hoping someone would defend you, and look what I found."

She leaned closer to read with him, head to head, and almost gasped. Someone had posted a rebuttal, all right. It read "Leave Baby Sister alone. Or else."

NINETEEN

By the time he had contacted headquarters and reported what he'd seen on the anonymous blog, Linc was fighting a terrible headache, probably partially due to his injury. He hadn't intended to tell Zoe he felt ill, but she must have sensed something off about him.

"Are you sure you're okay?" she asked for the third time when they got to her apartment.

"I told you I'm fine." The rebuttal came out stronger than he had wanted. "Sorry."

"See? That's what I mean. You're not acting like your normal self."

Arching a brow, he immediately regretted it because the pain intensified and he winced. "Oh, yeah?"

"Yeah." She came back from her kitchen with a glass of water and painkillers. "I'm not giving you aspirin in case your head damage is worse than the doctors thought. Take these and maybe your mood will improve."

Reluctantly, he did. "Thanks. I do have a slight headache."

"It's more than slight, but I won't argue as long as you take care of yourself."

Nodding carefully, Linc got to his feet. Star stirred,

lifted her head, then relaxed again and closed her eyes as if planning to spend the night.

"I probably should go," Linc said.

"Not on your life." Zoe was adamant. "Your relief is already parked out front. You're staying right here with me and Freddy so I can watch you for signs of a serious head injury."

"You're a doctor now?"

"Nope. A mother. We come with built-in sensitivity training. One look at you and I knew you felt rotten."

"I should be out looking for the RRK, not resting."

"Look." Facing him, Zoe placed a hand on his forearm. "I feel responsible for what happened to your head. And for what happened to Star the time before. You won't gain anything by chasing a mystery blogger's invisible fan in the middle of the night, even if he did sound like the RRK. Star can stay right where she is, and I've promised Freddy he can bring his blanket and pillow in here to camp out with the two of you. He's gone to pick out a stuffed animal to share with Star, too."

"Suppose there's a problem during the night?"

"With Security Forces visible outside and Star in here, I strongly doubt anybody will try anything. But I can tell Freddy that if the dog barks or growls, he has to come get me right away. He loves to have important jobs, so I'm sure he'll follow orders."

"Maybe I will rest here for a little while," Linc said. He sank onto the overstuffed sofa and laid his head back. "I am feeling pretty lousy."

"You may be hungry. All we had this afternoon was ice cream and cold pizza. How would you like some soup? I have vegetable and chicken noodle."

Freddy skipped into the room, his pudgy arms loaded with stuffed animals. "I love chicken noodle."

"Okay," Zoe said. "You guys make yourselves comfortable and I'll go open a can."

"Make sure the back door is locked," Linc called after her. He didn't hear a clear reply, but her tone was enough for him to tell she wasn't impressed with his suggestion. That was okay. He knew she'd already checked all the locks and was perfectly capable of taking care of such details. Habit and her enemy's efforts at making her look unstable had spurred him to speak up.

Freddy was standing at his feet, apparently waiting for an invitation to join him, so Linc patted the adjoining sofa cushion. "C'mon up, kid. And bring your friends."

Scrambling up with a small assist from Linc, the boy dumped his armload of toys in a cascade of synthetic fur.

Linc smiled. "Who all have we got here?"

"That's puppy one." He chose another. "This is puppy two."

Linc picked up a similar toy. "Is this puppy three?"

Freddy giggled. "No, Sergeant Linc. That's a kitty."

"Oh, sorry. My mistake."

"You can have her to sleep with if you want," Freddy offered. "She's a really good kitty. My favorite."

"Thank you." Linc couldn't help his growing smile. Freddy had not only presented him with a stuffed animal, he'd given his best. "That's very nice of you."

"You're welcome. I like you."

He ruffled the child's soft hair. "I like you, too."

"You like my mama?"

"Sure."

Apparently satisfied, the boy wiggled around, pushing aside toys, until he was snuggled tight against Linc's side and partially tucked beneath his arm. Then he yawned so loudly Star looked up to check on them.

"You go to sleep," Linc said. "I'm tired, too."

"Uh-huh. 'Night."

Leaning over slightly, despite the throbbing in his temples, Linc placed a kiss on the top of Freddy's head. "Good night, buddy."

When the boy snuggled even closer, laid a small arm part way across his ribs and whispered, "I love you," Linc was stunned. All his life he'd believed he disliked children, yet this one had punched a Texas-size hole in his opinion—and in his heart.

Leaning his head back again, Linc replied softly, "I love you, too, Freddy."

Zoe heated the soup then peeked in to ask Freddy and Linc if they wanted theirs in bowls at the table or in mugs they could sip from on the sofa. But she found them asleep. So was Star, who was snoring loudly.

Hesitant to disturb them, she gazed fondly at the scene of familial bliss. The only thing missing was her. In Zoe's eyes, she belonged on the opposite side of Linc, also snuggled close, to share in the perfect peace and trust her son was enjoying.

Instead, she returned to the kitchen and took the pot of soup off the stove. It would keep. So would her unacceptable dreams and wishes. Even if Linc did seem to be showing affection toward Freddy, she had to assume that feeling didn't extend to her. She was a job, a duty and an often-unpleasant one. If Linc and his fellow Security Forces members weren't after Boyd, they were chasing other bad guys, which had made her formerly stable life the subject of their ongoing investigations. Of course, Linc was here. Like the security team parked out in the street, he was actually working. And so was Star.

Zoe plopped down in a kitchen chair, elbows on the table, head in her hands, and let her mind drift like a plane in a holding pattern—until it touched down on solid ground and came to a screeching halt. What was that noise? Was Freddy ready to be put to bed? Had Linc stirred because he was unwell?

Rising as silently as possible, she tiptoed to the doorway to check on her guests. Star was the only one paying attention. Her head was raised, her ears forward, her nostrils twitching, seeking information available only to her keen canine senses.

Zoe was now certain that the sound she'd heard hadn't come from any of them. So what had disturbed her? She turned. Started back to the table. And spotted a piece of folded paper lying on the floor just inside her back door.

Eyes wide, she froze. How had someone bypassed the guard outside and got this close? Zoe stared at the note as if it were an angry Texas diamondback poised to strike. It may as well have been, given the effect it was having on her.

Trembling, she studied the double-locked door. Everything was intact. No one had tried to get in. But they had made it far enough to shake her world to its foundation.

She took a step closer and started to bend and reach for the piece of paper. But she stopped and made the kind of judgment a prey animal makes. The door was solid enough to deter rapid entry but probably not thick enough to stop a bullet. Maybe whoever had left that paper was still out there, gun aimed and hammer cocked, waiting for her to make a noise that would tell them it was time to act. To fire.

Trying to slow her rapid breathing, Zoe thought about grabbing a broom to retrieve the note by dragging it to her. Instead, she crouched and duckwalked out of the kitchen, not straightening until she was almost to the sofa. A light touch on Linc's arm brought him instantly awake and ready for battle.

"It's just me," she said, hands raised to deflect any instinctive efforts at self-defense.

"What's the matter?" He was scrubbing one hand over his face while the other palm rested on his sidearm.

"A note," Zoe whispered. "Somebody just shoved it under the back door and I didn't know what to do."

Linc immediately radioed the situation to the guard stationed outside, then commanded Star to watch the boy and made his way to the kitchen with Zoe.

She pointed. "There. See?"

The paper crackled when Linc picked it up. They heard movement on the deck. A board creaked. Something slid across the wood. A boot? A step?

Linc drew his gun. Frozen in place, they waited and listened for more.

A sharp knock and an all-clear call from the other guard came in seconds. It was only then that Zoe realized she'd been holding her breath.

TWENTY

Linc unfolded the note, holding it by the outer corners to preserve prints or other trace evidence. He actually considered keeping its contents from Zoe but decided she'd be safer if he kept her in the loop. He cleared his throat. "Somebody wants to meet with you tonight at the airfield."

"Who? Why?"

Nothing convinced him the single letter *B* signature was genuine or significant, so he said, "Doesn't matter. You're not going."

"Suppose it's my stalker. Or better yet, the RRK. You could set a trap and this would all be over."

"That's unacceptable."

"To you, maybe. Check with your superiors. They might have a different opinion. I'm not some clueless civilian. I'm air force, too, you know."

He pulled out his cell phone and photographed the note, then dialed Captain Blackwood's private number. "Colson here. I've just emailed you a note that was left at the Sullivan apartment, and I suggest our teams rendezvous at the airfield. Somebody is trying to lure Sergeant Sullivan out there and is telling her to come at 2200 hours."

"I see that. And I concur. Can she find a babysitter at this late hour?"

"She doesn't need to go," Linc countered.

"I think she does. We'll keep a close eye on her, but without her presence on scene, we'll have a slim chance of drawing out her stalker—or anybody else."

"But, sir—"

"No buts. I got the lab report on that piece of cloth your dog bit off at the day care. It came from a pair of Jim Ahern's coveralls. I was going to arrange to pick him up for questioning in the morning, but since this situation has come up, we may as well move in now."

"You think he's the one who sent this note?" Linc felt tension knotting his muscles.

"Who else could it be?"

"You got word about the blog posting, right?"

Blackwood huffed. "I did. It means nothing. Anybody could have written it, just like anybody could have signed your note with a *B*."

"You don't think it was Boyd Sullivan, then?"

"Not if he's as savvy as we think. Report to headquarters as soon as you find someone to watch the boy, or bring him with you if you can't. We'll assign an on-duty airman to babysit for as long as it takes to complete this operation."

"Yes, sir." Linc looked to Zoe and set his jaw. "Get your ABU and boots on. You're going with me."

Until Zoe was assured Freddy would be well cared for and fully protected by Security Forces, she was uncooperative. She didn't care how hard to handle she was; nobody was going to harm her little boy. Not on her watch.

They ended up placing Freddy within the K-9 unit, where he happily fell back to sleep in the company of a cuddly half-grown pup and a couple of armed night watchmen.

Linc handed her a Kevlar vest. "Put this on."

"Do you really think I'll need combat armor?"

"I'd rather you had it, okay? I let you come tonight, so humor me."

Zoe laughed. "*You* let me? Ha! I heard you talking to your captain. The only reason I'm here is for bait."

"Assistance."

"Okay, call it what you will. You know I volunteered to help regardless, so let's get this show on the road."

She allowed Linc to guide her as far as the exit, then struck out for his SUV on her own. Nobody was going to have reason to claim she was being coerced. Not if she had any say about it. Nor were they going to get away with staking her out like a hunk of dinner on a hungry tiger's jungle trail. She was in this up to her eyeballs and intended to participate to the best of her ability just as she did with every task she was assigned.

Yes, she was nervous. And, yes, she realized she was putting herself in harm's way. But as long as she was close to Linc Colson and Star, she felt safe enough to hold it together. If she'd been in the navy, she'd have called him her anchor.

The CAFB airfield was so well lit there wasn't a lot of difference between night and day except for swirling clouds of orange dust that dimmed the beams cast by overhead vapor lights. Captain Blackwood's attack plan had placed hidden forces in two concentric circles with

Linc and Star taking point. Zoe was ordered to wait in his vehicle, out of the substantial wind, until called for.

Linc realized he was fighting more than one battle and struggled to concentrate on the task at hand while his heart and mind remained with Zoe. How could she purposely endanger herself like this? She'd seemed so sensible, so clever to begin with.

The only thing that helped him cope was knowing that Captain Blackwood had already sent men to take Jim Ahern into custody at his home. Once they reported success, there would be far less to worry about. That was good, because right now Linc was pretty distracted despite his vow to remain totally professional.

"Which increases the danger, because I'm not thinking straight," he murmured. That was bad. If he did nothing more tonight, he must somehow set aside his angst before it got him, or somebody else, killed.

Allowing himself one quick glance at Zoe through the car windows, he gave her a thumbs-up sign.

"Colson in position," Linc radioed his teammates, keeping his back to the prevailing wind so it wouldn't blow directly into the mic and distort communications.

Blackwood's voice was strong and sure. "Stay alert. Ahern was not at home, so he's probably here. Be careful. We want him alive."

"Affirmative."

With Star on a short leash, Linc started to work his way toward the base of the control tower where the note had instructed Zoe to meet.

Merely thinking her name made his gut knot and his palms sweat. A long, slow blink and a sigh were meant to clear his mind and sharpen his wits.

Star paused in her stride just enough to alert him.

Before he could react, the snap, whine and echo of a rifle shot sliced the night air. Linc felt the disturbance near his ear and knew he had just been shot at. And missed. Barely.

He hit the tarmac with his shoulder and rolled, ending in a crouch and scrambling for cover behind a maintenance truck, Star at his side.

He heard Blackwood in his radio and replied, "No, Captain. I wasn't hit. Did anybody see where the shot came from?"

"Negative, Colson. Hold your position."

"Yes, sir." Linc kept Star close. He didn't intend to survive combat with his K-9 and then let some idiot with a rifle take them out on their home turf. "No wonder they couldn't find Ahern at his quarters. He's here."

Blackwood's reply was unsettling at the very least. "He's here, all right, but that wasn't him shooting at you. We caught him selling marijuana in one of the hangars. He's been in custody for several minutes."

"Really? Maybe it's the woman we suspected of knocking me over the head behind the preschool."

"Or Sullivan is back."

Linc's throat threatened to close. "Is that possible? I thought he was spotted at Baylor."

"He's been seen a lot of places, but nobody has proved any of it. Just keep your eyes open and your head down."

"Yes, sir. Has anybody got Ahern to talk?"

"Negative. He still denies involvement in the stalking incidents," Blackwood answered.

"Copy." Despite the wind that swirled dirt and sand around him, Linc was able to see enough of the runways and tower to feel fairly secure where he was. Security

Forces had the tower surrounded and the controllers secured, hopefully trapping the shooter inside their temporary perimeter with no opportunity to foul up landings and takeoffs. Now, they'd rely on the dust to mask their possible approach and wait for orders to close the net.

Star's ears perked up. Sensing danger, Linc started to stand. Another rifle shot sounded and he ducked back, only to realize the shooter had not aimed for him this time. Zoe was his target! And there was a hole punched through the windshield right where she had been sitting.

Zoe slipped out of Linc's damaged vehicle and lowered herself onto the tarmac, staying behind the open door as much as possible. "Father, please protect the good guys, especially Linc. Please."

Boots and camo-covered legs appeared beside her. She recognized Ethan Webb when he asked, "You hit?"

"No." Good thing she'd been hunched down in the seat. "Is Linc okay?"

"Yeah." Ethan's rifle was held at the ready, his gaze moving over the surrounding area while he radioed a report of her condition.

"It has to be my stalker who's shooting," Zoe said. "I told Linc I wanted to go meet him face-to-face, so we could avoid this kind of thing."

"Might not have mattered in the long run. We already took Ahern into custody."

"Then who just shot at me?"

"No idea." He frowned at her. "You have a little boy, Sergeant. Why are you out here risking your life?"

"Captain Blackwood wanted me here," she said without hesitation. "But I expected to take a more active role."

Zoe saw the lieutenant rise to one knee and assume a defensive pose, rifle ready, as someone else approached.

Nobody had to tell Zoe who it was. She could sense Linc was coming just as well as his K-9 sensed trouble.

Linc had stayed low, taking evasive action while moving toward better shelter. His fear was magnified by concern for Zoe and he demonstrated it clearly when he darted behind the SUV to join her and Ethan.

Ignoring the other man, he glared at Zoe. "I thought I told you to stay put."

"I did—until somebody punched a hole through the window."

Ethan Webb interrupted. "You two can argue later when all this is over. Right now, we have other concerns." He was scowling, and Linc realized he was right.

"Sorry, Lieutenant. Any word on who's doing the shooting?"

"Apparently whoever was working with Ahern. We have people closing in."

"Copy that." Linc quieted to listen to his radio. "Sounds like we have a woman in custody. They're requesting backup."

Ethan nodded. "You have the attack dog, Colson, so you take it. I'll go report to Captain Blackwood."

Linc saluted. "Yes, sir."

Frowning, angry and so frustrated he wanted to shout at everything and nothing, Linc turned to Zoe. "Get in the vehicle, lock the doors and keep your head down. I'll be back ASAP."

Her "Yes, Sergeant" did not sound particularly amiable, but he was willing to settle for any kind of compliance that would guarantee her safety.

Waiting for her to climb into the SUV and follow his orders, he was satisfied. There had been no more shooting and his fellow team members were getting the situation in hand. Even if Ahern wouldn't talk, Linc hoped his cohort would.

Broken-field running took Linc and Star to Westley James and his K-9, Dakota, where they stood with other Security Forces members. Sure enough, they had nabbed a woman dressed in all black. Linc recognized her, helped by her red hair. "That's Anne McNally."

"Who?" the sergeant asked.

"The airman who was offered to assist me in a computer search. Zoe was suspicious, but I put off checking because McNally had been spoken for by Captain Blackwood." He confronted the handcuffed woman. "How long have you and Ahern been working together?"

All she did was laugh. "Get real. Do you think I'm so desperate I'd need to sink to his level to get a date?"

"It's too late to try to divert suspicion," Linc said. "He's already been arrested."

McNally shrugged. "Why should I care?"

Linc clenched his fists. He looked to Westley. "What about it, Sarge? What do you think?"

"I'm not sure. We caught her hiding over there with a handheld radio but didn't see a rifle."

"It's around. We'll find it."

"What about your suspicions regarding Boyd Sullivan?" Sergeant James asked. "What's up with him?"

"All I know is that he or someone posing as him posted a response on the anonymous blog, and Zoe got a note signed with the letter *B*. I suppose it could be Boyd, but if it is, he's getting sloppy."

"I agree."

Still on alert, Linc checked their surroundings and perceived no threat. "Do you want me to deliver her to the captain or will you do the honors?"

"You take her," Sergeant James said. "Dakota and I were assigned this quadrant, so I'll stay at my post."

Linc nodded, grabbed the red-haired woman's arm and pulled her to her feet. She smelled of liquor. "Get moving."

Anne gave an annoying giggle and threw herself against Linc's chest as if accidentally losing her balance. "Oops. You mean you aren't going to pitch me over your shoulder and carry me?" Her speech slurred. "What a pity. I was looking forward to a little macho action."

Linc righted her and held her away as they walked. "I'd sooner kiss a rattlesnake."

No matter how hard Zoe peered into the dust-clouded night she couldn't see far enough to observe Linc. That was not only frustrating to her but it set her nerves on edge even more. Darkness didn't frighten her. Neither did being alone. There was just something comforting about being able to see Linc—and Star. And something unexplainably unsettling when she couldn't.

She shivered. The wind's velocity seemed to be picking up, as if the very weather sensed her unrest. That was ridiculous, of course, but it wasn't too far-fetched to think that she might be tuning in to the turbulent atmosphere outside the SUV.

Bursts of sand and pebbles peppered the windows. Zoe cringed, thankful that the bullet had struck the windshield. Its laminated construction kept the glass in one piece, although there was a pea-size hole just off center with spiderweb-looking lines radiating from it like a sunburst.

She fixated on that damage, realizing how close she had come to being killed, and whispered, "Thank You, Jesus."

Her seat seemed to vibrate as gusts rocked the vehicle. Zoe closed her eyes and said an ongoing prayer of thanksgiving, adding pleas for the safety of everyone involved. To her surprise, she even found herself mentioning her nefarious brother. He had caused so much trouble, so much pain, yet she still recalled their childhood and the protective older sibling he had been then, despite his unruly nature. There had to be some good in him. There simply had to be.

Suddenly, the window beside her head shattered into a million pieces, the tiny shards covering her like the blowing Texas sand. Instinct made her cover her face.

Not prone to screaming when startled, Zoe hesitated long enough to feel herself being grabbed and pulled through the opening of the now-missing side window. Stretching her arm and shoulder sent sharp pain all the way down her spine and her ribs banged against the window's lower edge.

That was enough impetus to set her off. She took the deepest breath she could and let loose with a yowl that would have done the scream queen of a scary movie proud. The assailant pulled her into a bear hug and cut off the screech.

Everything was happening so fast that Zoe couldn't tell who had hold of her or what he was planning, but she did know one thing—anyone who would cause this kind of pain was capable of almost anything.

The wind whipped her hair across her face and sand stung her exposed skin, but that was nothing compared to the severe way she was being held, arms pinned at her sides, hot breath so close to her face that she couldn't turn her head.

Tears blurred her vision. Unable to free a hand to rub her eyes, she blinked rapidly and tried to focus. "Let me go."

His response sent chills up her spine. He laughed and the sound was pure evil.

Through her fear, she heard something familiar. She recognized that voice. Michael Orleck. Her washed-out student. He was behind all the assaults and stalking?

"You!" Zoe gasped.

Orleck laughed again. "Took you long enough. I figured you'd be deemed unfit and drummed out of the air force a lot sooner than this. You're a disappointment, *Teacher*."

"*That's* why you've been making my life miserable? I thought you were happy repairing planes."

"That's what I wanted everybody to think." He kept hold of one of her arms and with his other hand he reached for the rifle that had been slung across his back. "You ruined my life. I figured it was only fair to return the favor."

"You're crazy."

"Maybe. But I'm not the one calling security day after day because I'm imagining prowlers and dirty tricks and outright attacks. I'm also not the one being blamed for letting a serial killer sneak onto the base and murder innocent airmen."

"That's not true, and you know it."

"I don't know anything of the kind, Teacher. Have you read the base blog lately?"

"That was you?"

"I made a few comments, yes."

Stalling for time and hoping that someone would notice her plight and send help, Zoe kept him talking. "How did you know?"

"Know what?"

"To call me Baby Sister."

"Ah, that."

He hesitated just long enough to cause her to wonder if Boyd might actually have posted the cryptic warning.

"I worked with an old buddy of your brother's, you know. I heard things."

She tried to free her arm, but his vise grip tightened instead. "You're hurting me."

"Tough. You think you're so smart, so perfect. Well, I've outsmarted you and that cop boyfriend of yours. Now I'm going to fix you for good and blame it on your crazy brother."

She made a monumental effort to escape, kicking at him and throwing her weight in the opposite direction. Thanks to her self-defense training, she managed to loosen his grip on her arm. But only for a second.

Recovering and lunging, Orleck clamped both hands around her throat. He grimaced and tightened the stranglehold. She wanted to scream again, to call out to Linc, but she couldn't get enough air.

Zoe felt herself losing consciousness. Would help arrive in time? She managed to choke out a raspy "Jesus, help me," before the attacker cut off the last of her air.

TWENTY-ONE

Star alerted, her focus on where Linc had left Zoe, shortly after he'd delivered McNally to Blackwood.

Linc noticed and tensed. "Captain?"

"Yes?"

"Star's acting strange. Permission to return to Sergeant Sullivan?"

"Permission granted. As soon as we locate the missing weapon and make sure this incident is over, we'll wrap up and head back."

"Yes, sir."

Whirling, Linc loosened the lead to give his dog plenty of slack. She took it immediately, straining and beginning to bark. He followed at a run until they were within sight of the SUV. Two figures stood beside it, blurred by shadows and the swirling dust. It looked as if they were struggling.

His gut told him the same thing his K-9 had been insisting: Zoe was in trouble. If he charged into the fray as his heart kept insisting, there was a strong possibility she'd end up being harmed. However, if he trusted his K-9's judgment, the chances of successfully capturing her assailant were much better. Star knew Zoe. She wouldn't make a mistake when choosing between good and evil. She'd bite the bad guy.

He reeled Star in and unclipped her leash, keeping hold of her collar and peering at the altercation still taking place. It was now or never. Simultaneously letting go of her collar, he shouted, "Get 'em," and began to run.

Barking ferociously, Star quickly outpaced him and rounded the parked truck. He heard a human shout coupled with intense growling.

"Good girl. Hold 'em," Linc yelled, knowing Star was biting her target.

When Linc slid to a stop at the other side of the truck, Star had Michael Orleck's forearm in her teeth. The K-9 was being lifted off the ground as her quarry screamed and struggled to shake her off, but she held firm.

What about Zoe? Linc spotted her and reached out, barely in time to catch her before she collapsed. He wrapped his arms around her, her head falling back over his arm, and he silently prayed he hadn't been too late.

Had he lost his love before he'd had a chance to admit how he felt about her—and Freddy?

Finally, she drew a shuddering breath. Then another. Tears filled his eyes and gratitude his heart. This time, God had heard him. This time, the answer was clear.

It took Linc several more moments to realize that Star had moved from the arm to the seat of the mechanic's coveralls. Pieces of the puzzle started to fall into place. Things Anne McNally had said made sense now. She had been helping Orleck, not Ahern, and chances were good that the crime lab would find DNA from both men on the scrap of fabric Star had torn away from the older mechanic's stolen coveralls.

Linc looked down at Zoe and his hand touched her cheek, just as Captain Blackwood drew up next to him.

"She needs to go to the ER."

"I know, Captain. She's started breathing again, but she should be checked out."

"What happened?"

"Orleck was choking her. Star is holding him for us."

The captain looked as though he wanted to grin. "I see. Better give your dog the release command before she tears the jumpsuit off him. We'll take over. You get the sergeant to our standby ambulance. I'll check in with you at the hospital."

Zoe stirred in Linc's arms, and he pulled her across his chest in a more comfortable carrying position. He rained kisses on her hair and let his tears of absolute relief slide silently down his cheeks as he carried her toward the waiting ambulance.

Zoe opened her eyes and struggled to speak. Her throat was so tight, the muscles in her neck and shoulders so sore that she failed. This wasn't a dream. Linc was carrying her. He'd come in time. Praise the Lord! She didn't know how close she'd come to dying but had a sense it had been imminent.

There was something important she needed to tell him. She tried to raise her head. When he looked down at her, he was smiling. And his eyes were glistening. She had to speak. To tell him about Orleck.

"It was…"

Instead of listening, Linc gently kissed her.

"No, no." She managed a weak shake of her head.

"I'm sorry. I wasn't going to do that until I could ask first. I'm so happy you're going to be okay. I slipped up." He sobered. "Won't happen again."

"No." This time there was an underlying sob in her voice. Her palm rested on his chest, and she could feel the pounding of his heart. His dear heart. "I...tell... you..."

"Ah." Linc seemed to understand because his tender expression returned. "You want to tell me who the real stalker was."

"Uh-huh."

"It's okay, honey. We got him. Or Star did. Didn't you see and hear her attacking? She was amazing."

A sense of relief beyond anything she'd ever imagined bathed Zoe in calm as Linc held her close and strode across the tarmac, carrying her as if she didn't weigh an ounce. "Star is okay?"

"She's fine," he assured her, as he placed her on a gurney near the rear of an ambulance.

While medics checked her vital signs, he held her hand. "Don't try to talk anymore now. There'll be plenty of time after you've recovered."

"I didn't get out, honest." Her throat burned, yet she tried to continue explaining. "He pulled me through the window and—"

Linc gently placed two fingers over her mouth, following the movement of the gurney as the medics rolled it.

"You riding along, Sarge?" one of the medics asked.

"Me and the dog," Linc said flatly. Star had rejoined him at his side. "Your patient is an important witness and I need to debrief her ASAP." He leaned over the gurney and whispered into Zoe's ear, "I also need to kiss her again, if she ever stops talking long enough."

Smiling through the tears and lingering pain, Zoe went silent, then pointed to her closed mouth.

This time, she didn't get the simple token of affection she'd expected. Linc's kiss was so perfect, so wondrous, so filled with love she was overcome. Closing her eyes, she returned his feelings completely, committing her heart without another word. Never in her whole life, including the time she'd been married, had she been so moved, so emotionally connected to anyone.

Her arms encircled his neck, holding him close, until he gently unwound them and eased away. Zoe looked up and saw him smile. Sensed the depth of his sincerity when he whispered, "I love you."

"I love you, too."

Linc was kicked back in a sickly green plastic-covered hospital chair next to Zoe's bed, Star at his feet, when his captain entered the curtained cubicle.

Linc started to rise. Blackwood waved him back down. "As you were."

"Did he confess?" Linc saw Captain Blackwood's gaze shift to Zoe. She was hooked up to oxygen via a nasal cannula, so her face was visible.

"Yes, Orleck admitted everything."

Linc heard Zoe sigh with relief. "That's good," he said to the captain, reaching for Zoe's hand and giving it an affectionate squeeze. "What about Ahern?"

"Apparently innocent, at least of bothering Sergeant Sullivan. He may be a drug peddler but he isn't a stalker."

"Orleck admitted it all? Even how he managed to set up the warehouse fiasco?"

"Yes." Blackwood turned to Zoe. "He and McNally had been following you, hoping to stage their fake shooting where you'd be the only one to see it so they could make you look crazy. Ducking into that warehouse provided a perfect staging area."

"What about the fake blood?" Linc asked.

"He used a squib, same as they do in the movies. The mess was contained by her shirt."

Linc was frowning. "What was his reasoning for going to all that trouble?"

"He wanted everybody to believe Zoe was mentally unbalanced and should be relieved of duty," Blackwood explained. "They used that same fake blood stuff in her bedroom, just like the lab reported."

Linc felt Zoe's fingers tighten around his and squeezed back for moral support. "How about access? How did he get into her apartment?"

"Airman McNally handled master keys in the course of her duty, so that was all he needed. He admitted to entering the apartment multiple times, including hiding while Portia babysat. I'm glad he stayed out of sight until she left."

Zoe found her voice then. "That was him?"

"Yes," Blackwood said flatly. "Some of the other things he tried may not have come to light yet, but he swears his intentions weren't lethal—until tonight." He stepped closer to Zoe. "You can go home whenever you're ready. Your duty schedule is being adjusted to give you several more weeks off with pay, so you can recuperate."

Her "Thank you, sir" was hoarse, raspy and sounded very emotional. "If they keep me here, I'll need someone to watch Freddy."

"I can help do that," Linc said. "And we can always let him go back to his regular schedule if I need to work."

"I can't ask you to do that," Zoe insisted. Trying to speak louder brought on a coughing fit. Linc got to his feet and handed her a glass of ice water. Their hands didn't just brush in passing as he kept hold of the plastic tumbler and she cupped her fingers over his.

Justin Blackwood cleared his throat. "Yes, well, I can see it's high time I gave you two some privacy. Take care of yourself, Sergeant Sullivan. Your life should quiet down now."

Linc waited until the curtains closed behind his commanding officer before settling a hip on the side of the narrow cot. He set the water tumbler aside and grasped both of Zoe's hands. "I know how you can feel even safer. Freddy, too."

"Oh? Do you plan to bring Star and crash on my sofa for the rest of my life?"

"Something like that." He paused, blaming the tightness in his own throat on empathy for her. "I—I thought you might like to get married."

Zoe gasped. "Married?"

"Uh-huh. You know the drill. White dress, church, flowers, the whole nine yards."

"You want to marry *me*?"

He grinned at her, wondering if she was truly as shocked as she pretended to be. "Yeah. I'm as surprised as you are. It kind of sneaked up on me."

Zoe's eyes glistened. "What did?"

"Love. I fought against my feelings for you as long as I could, but when I heard that shot and saw it hit right where I thought you were sitting, I had to admit how deeply I cared. I love everything about you."

"Including my son?"

"Especially him." Linc raised their joined hands and kissed hers. "I know this is sudden, and you're not deathly afraid of the Red Rose Killer the way other people are, but I'd still like the chance to stay close to you, to protect and look after you and Freddy."

"Only if you stop seeing me as a needy victim and take me as a life partner," Zoe whispered. "I don't want to be an extension of your job. I want to be your wife."

"You do?"

"Yes. I do. I don't know how long I've been in love with you, but I knew we were right for each other even before I admitted it to myself."

"When do you want to schedule the wedding?" Linc asked, assuming she would put him off for a reasonable amount of time rather than rush into anything as important as marriage.

"I had the lacy white gown once," she said tenderly. "If we wear our dress uniforms, we can get Pastor Harmon to make it official in his church office as soon as possible."

"You don't want time to plan a big party?"

"Those are mostly for friends and family. I don't need that," Zoe said, giving Linc a smile that melted his heart. "Star can be my maid of honor and a member of Security Forces can be your best man. We can get Felicity to take pictures, too. She and Westley married quickly, so I'm sure she'd be delighted to help us do the same."

Linc had to laugh. "I've just proposed and already you have the whole ceremony planned."

"It pays to be organized," she replied, freeing her hands from his and opening her arms. "How about a kiss to seal the bargain?"

"How about more than one?"

"Works for me," Zoe said, blushing.

Linc was more than happy to oblige.

EPILOGUE

Ethan Webb barged into Pastor Harmon's office in time to watch Linc bend Zoe backward over his arm like an iconic photo and kiss his bride with gusto.

Zoe blushed, Freddy giggled and applauded, Star barked and others in the small intimate gathering laughed. Linc righted her, grinning at the lieutenant. "You missed it, Ethan."

"I caught the best part. My apologies to both of you. I was stuck on the phone with my former father-in-law. Looks like my K-9 and I are going to be loaned to Baylor Marine Base after all."

"That's tough," Linc said. "I probably shouldn't mention exes at my own wedding, but I hope yours doesn't drive you crazy while you're over there."

"Not a chance. I'll be assigned to work with her father, Lieutenant Colonel Masters, not Jillian. I'll manage."

Zoe reached out her hand and laid it gently on his uniform sleeve. "Linc told me a little about your problems and why you're being sent to Baylor. We'll pray for your safety and success."

She saw the lieutenant pause to glance from her to Linc and back again before he asked, "Both of you?"

Linc nodded. "Yes. I finally woke up and realized it

wasn't God who had abandoned me, it was I who had left Him."

It warmed Zoe's heart to see the relief and joy on Ethan's face. She shared his sentiment. Stumbling through life without faith was possible of course, but with it, her view of everything had changed. She'd even been able to forgive her brother up to a point. She did love the person Boyd had once been, the little boy who had done his best to survive in the toxic environment of their family home. Now she knew there was sadly no going back for Boyd and had accepted the inevitable.

Freed, in a way, she would go forward with her husband and her son. The best was yet to come for them. Starting right now. She slipped both arms around Linc's neck, stood on tiptoe and smiled through a mist of happy tears. "I think Felicity missed getting a picture of our wedding kiss when it was cut short. We need to repeat it."

Linc didn't argue. As cameras, as well as cell phones, clicked, he gave his new bride exactly what she'd asked for—and more. He kissed her until they were both breathless, then bent to scoop up Freddy and included the laughing child in a group hug.

Zoe was so happy her tears flowed. It was official. They were a real family.

* * * * *

Dear Reader,

This is a story of redemption and forgiveness. Even when our past is troubled, there is always hope, always a way to go on. Personally, I don't know how anyone copes daily without a saving faith in Jesus Christ. He has brought me through many trials when I saw only dark clouds and imagined no rainbows, no possibilities of future happiness.

The struggles of Zoe and Linc were intensified because they both dwelled on an unhappy past rather than accepting the new chance for love that was awaiting them. We can't go back and fix mistakes—and would probably make things worse if we tried. Each challenge is a way to learn and grow, each new day a precious gift. We only need to accept God's love and forgiveness, trust Him and willingly place the rest of our lives in His care.

I can be reached by email at Val@ValerieHansen.com, or via my website, www.ValerieHansen.com.

Blessings,
Valerie

Get 4 FREE REWARDS!

We'll send you 2 FREE Books plus 2 FREE Mystery Gifts.

Love Inspired® Suspense books feature Christian characters facing challenges to their faith... and lives.

FREE Value Over $20

YES! Please send me 2 FREE Love Inspired® Suspense novels and my 2 FREE mystery gifts (gifts are worth about $10 retail). After receiving them, if I don't wish to receive any more books, I can return the shipping statement marked "cancel." If I don't cancel, I will receive 4 brand-new novels every month and be billed just $5.24 each for the regular-print edition or $5.74 each for the larger-print edition in the U.S., or $5.74 each for the regular-print edition or $6.24 each for the larger-print edition in Canada. That's a savings of at least 13% off the cover price. It's quite a bargain! Shipping and handling is just 50¢ per book in the U.S. and 75¢ per book in Canada*. I understand that accepting the 2 free books and gifts places me under no obligation to buy anything. I can always return a shipment and cancel at any time. The free books and gifts are mine to keep no matter what I decide.

Choose one: ☐ **Love Inspired® Suspense Regular-Print** (153/353 IDN GMY5)   ☐ **Love Inspired® Suspense Larger-Print** (107/307 IDN GMY5)

Name (please print)

Address   Apt. #

City   State/Province   Zip/Postal Code

Mail to the Reader Service:
IN U.S.A.: P.O. Box 1341, Buffalo, NY 14240-8531
IN CANADA: P.O. Box 603, Fort Erie, Ontario L2A 5X3

Want to try two free books from another series? Call 1-800-873-8635 or visit www.ReaderService.com.

First Lieutenant Ethan Webb brushed past the startled aide standing in Colonel Masters's outer office.

"The colonel is—"

"Waiting for me," Ethan snapped. "I know." Lt. Col. Terence Masters, Ethan's former father-in-law, was always a step ahead of him. He led Titus, his German shorthaired pointer, into the office, found Masters seated in his leather chair.

"You're late," Masters said. "And I don't want your dog in here."

"With respect, sir, the dog goes where I go, and I don't appreciate you pressuring my commanding officer to get me to do this harebrained job during my leave. I said I would consider it, didn't I?"

"A little extra insurance to help you make up your mind, Webb."

"It's a bad idea. Leave me alone to do my investigation with the team at Canyon, and we'll catch Sullivan." They were working around the clock to put away the serial killer who was targeting his air force brothers and sisters as well as a few select others, including Ethan's ex-wife, Jillian.

"Your team," Masters said, "hasn't gotten the job done, and this lunatic has threatened my daughter. You're going to work for me privately, protect Jillian from Sullivan, draw him out and catch him, as we've discussed."

"So you think I'm going to pretend to be married to Jillian again and that's going to put us in the perfect position to catch Sullivan?" He shoved a hand through his crew-cut hair, striving for control. "This is lunacy. I can't believe you're willing to use your daughter as bait."

"I'm not," he said. "I've decided it's too risky for Jillian, and that's why I hired this girl. This is Kendra Bell."

The civilian woman stepped into the office and Ethan could only stare at her.

"You're..." He shook himself slightly and tried again. "I mean... You look like..."

"Your ex-wife," she finished. "I know. That's the point."

Don't miss
TOP SECRET TARGET by Dana Mentink,
available June 2018 wherever
Love Inspired® Suspense books and ebooks are sold.

www.LoveInspired.com

Looking for inspiration in tales
of hope, faith and heartfelt romance?

Check out **Love Inspired**® and
Love Inspired® **Suspense** books!

New books available every month!

_____

CONNECT WITH US AT:

Harlequin.com/Community

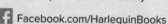 Facebook.com/HarlequinBooks

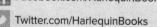 Twitter.com/HarlequinBooks

 Instagram.com/HarlequinBooks

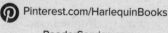 Pinterest.com/HarlequinBooks

ReaderService.com

Love Inspired®

LIGENRE2018